The
Serpent
Rider

The Serpent Rider

Yxavel Magno Diño

BLOOMSBURY
CHILDREN'S BOOKS
NEW YORK   LONDON   OXFORD   NEW DELHI   SYDNEY

BLOOMSBURY CHILDREN'S BOOKS
Bloomsbury Publishing Inc., part of Bloomsbury Publishing Plc
1385 Broadway, New York, NY 10018

BLOOMSBURY, BLOOMSBURY CHILDREN'S BOOKS, and the Diana logo are trademarks of
Bloomsbury Publishing Plc

First published in the United States of America in September 2024
by Bloomsbury Children's Books
www.bloomsbury.com

Bloomsbury books may be purchased for business or promotional use. For information on
bulk purchases please contact Macmillan Corporate and Premium Sales Department at
specialmarkets@macmillan.com

Library of Congress Cataloging-in-Publication Data
available upon request
ISBN 978-1-5476-1513-1 (hardcover) • ISBN 978-1-5476-1514-8 (e-book)
ISBN 978-1-5476-1790-6 (AUS)

Book design by Yelena Safronova
Typeset by Westchester Publishing Services
Printed and bound in the U.S.A.
2 4 6 8 10 9 7 5 3 1

To find out more about our authors and books visit www.bloomsbury.com
and sign up for our newsletters.

For Elyxa and Yxaak

The
Serpent
Rider

Chapter 1

My sister told me there had once been seven moons. But now, only one watched me from the night sky as I fought a battle I couldn't lose.

I leaped out of the way as my opponent's twin swords scythed toward me. Then he attacked again, faster this time. If I'd jumped back just a heartbeat later, I would have been skewered.

"You're too slow, Tani." Bato laughed. "You'll have to be faster than that to beat me."

I scowled. "I'm just warming up."

Little did he know I had a few tricks of my own.

Instead of attacking, I dug my blade into the sand and flicked it upward. Bato flinched as wet sand sprayed into his face.

While he was distracted, I rained down a flurry of blows, my movements as fluid as water. With my instincts honed by Swordmaster Pai's endless drills in the traditional war form—spinning, leaping, and striking with our blades as fast as the wind—battling felt more like dancing to me than fighting.

But Bato had been through the exact same training. And he had a weapon that was far deadlier than my sword.

Bato fell back before my relentless attack, still swiping sand from his eyes. But before I could take the victory, he let out a piercing whistle.

A sinuous, serpentine creature appeared at Bato's side, her coppery scales shining in the moonlight. The creature coiled back, ready to strike—then with a flick of her finned tail, sent a blast of fire roaring toward me.

I dropped into a roll as the sand behind me sizzled. Gasping, I let go of my sword as the iron glowed red-hot. Then Bato shoved me hard. I reeled backward and fell onto my behind.

My muscles bunched, and I was ready to leap back into the fight—but Bato stepped forward and rested the tip of his sword right above my heart.

"Yield," he said, smirking.

I glared at him as heat rose to my cheeks. If only my anger was as sharp as his knives, I'd have beaten him a thousand times already.

Finally, I sighed. "Yield," I muttered under my breath.

Bato laughed. "For someone who's supposed to be our 'destined hero,' you're pretty easy to defeat, aren't you?"

He offered me a hand to help me to my feet, but I scowled

and got up myself, walking past him to retrieve my sword. Of all people, I couldn't believe I'd let myself lose to *him*.

Bato shrugged, still smiling. "Great work, Iska." At the sound of her name, the copper-scaled creature drifted over to her master and hissed appreciatively as Bato patted her scales.

Iska was a bakunawa: a flying serpent with the magical ability to control the elements. Iska had the power to breathe fire, which—as I'd once again found out—could be devastating in a fight.

Bato and Iska weren't the only formidable pair. All the novices training tonight had a magnificent bakunawa of their own. Everyone except me.

Well, *almost* everyone.

My cheeks still burning from how quickly I'd lost, I made my way through the sparring area where more warriors-in-training pitted their strength and skill against each other.

Pairs of fighters lunged, ducked, and rolled, while above them, their bakunawa twisted and coiled like bright metallic ribbons. In one square, a blaze of fire from one bakunawa was held at bay by a curtain of water summoned by another. In the square beside them, a fighter barely managed to avoid being pummeled by rocks as his bakunawa scattered them with a blast of wind.

Black sand crunched beneath my feet as I headed toward the old seawall, where defeated fighters sat until sparring practice was over. Before the others' bakunawa hatched, I was never the first to get there. But now, I spent more time sitting and watching than fighting.

A lone figure perched atop the seawall waved at me. He was short and skinny, his heels swinging against the salt-bleached stone.

"Hey, Kiri." I dropped beside him with a sigh. "How long did you last?"

"Fifteen seconds." Kiri gave a lopsided smile, combing a hand through his mop of dark hair. "I saw you did better, though."

"Not by much. Bato and Iska took me out pretty fast."

As we spoke, Bato began to spar with the fighter who had beaten Kiri—a lanky kid with an air bakunawa. Swordmaster Pai organized our training into a tournament-like style, with the loser of each pair being eliminated until there was only one fighter left: the victor.

Kiri and I had long given up on being the victor. Just like mine, Kiri's bakunawa hadn't hatched yet, meaning we were both on the bottom.

In Kalinawan, every child born under the Warrior's Star was given a bakunawa egg at birth, collected by the village healer from a sacred pool. The creature within the egg would grow along with the child until they started warrior training at the age of ten. That was around the same time that the bakunawa egg would hatch, and the child and their bakunawa would form an unbreakable bond that would last for a lifetime.

But having a legendary serpent creature as your faithful

companion wasn't just for show. The forest around our village teemed with dark enchantments and wicked beasts, and our warriors—known as Serpent Riders—needed supernatural beings of their own to fight the creatures that threatened the safety of our people.

I thumped my fist against the seawall. "I just wish our bakunawa would hatch already so I can punch Bato's arrogant smile right into his arrogant face."

Kiri winced. "I'm excited too," he said, "because I want to meet my new friend. What kind do you think yours is?"

I thought for a moment. "I think my bakunawa will be a fire one."

"That would suit you." Kiri nodded. "I'm hoping mine will be air."

An air bakunawa would match Kiri perfectly—my friend was so skinny, the faintest puff of wind could knock him over. And yet, he was the only person who didn't find Bato totally infuriating. I'd *never* seen him get angry—even when his opponents knocked him flat on his back five times in a row.

With my tall and muscular build, the two of us couldn't have been more different. In another life, we might not have been friends, but our shared losses brought us together. We shared an unrelenting determination to give everything our best, even when the odds were stacked against us. Because of that, we always stood up for each other no matter what.

Noticing my stormy expression, Kiri smiled. "In a fair fight, though, you'd beat Bato any day."

Kiri was right. Before anyone's bakunawa had hatched, when we sparred with blades only, I *always* won. Even Bato hadn't been able to beat me.

But no matter how good I was with my sword, there was no way an iron weapon could defend against the bakunawa's magical attacks. Without a bakunawa of my own, I'd quickly gone from being the top novice warrior to one of the worst. And that knowledge hurt more than any bruise I'd ever get in training.

While Kiri and I had been talking, more defeated fighters had joined us on the seawall. Now there were only two novices left on the practice ground—Bato and a girl who was built like a water buffalo. The pair exchanged furious blows, while above, Iska and the other bakunawa spat fire and water, each serpent trying to gain the upper hand.

Finally, Iska had the water bakunawa wrapped tight in her coils. At the same time, Bato lunged toward his opponent, disarming her easily. The stocky girl lifted her hands in surrender.

"The victor!" someone shouted. "Bato!"

Along the seawall, others took up the cheer.

Bato raised his arms in triumph as he soaked up the praise. Iska wrapped protectively around him, the serpent's intelligent eyes flashing gold like twin suns. She had hatched two years ago, and now Iska was big enough for Bato to ride.

"Hey, Kiri and Tani," Bato called with a wave. "Did you two have a good rest?"

My fists clenched, but Kiri placed a hand on my arm to

stop me from rising to the bait. I hated how easily Bato could provoke my infamous temper—especially since he was as stubborn as his name, which meant "rock." Even though I knew Bato won the challenge fairly, a selfish part of me couldn't help but think that I should've been standing in his place.

On the other side of the training ground, Swordmaster Pai brought his hands together, halting the session. He smiled at Bato like a proud grandfather looking upon his favorite grandchild.

Swordmaster Pai was a fearsome warrior. His bakunawa, Talas, died in a battle many years ago, but he'd had the serpent's scales crafted into special armor that was stronger than iron. Whenever he wore the armor, it was like Talas was still protecting him.

Now that sparring was over, Swordmaster Pai called us back to the lesson hall for supper, where little kids ladled sticky rice into plates made of hollow bamboo stems. I usually loved sticky rice, but right now I didn't think I could stand another hour of Bato crowing in my face.

"Enjoy the food," I replied to Kiri's questioning look. "I'll see you tomorrow."

Leaving the beach, I headed up the rocky, moonlit path back to the village. All the houses in Kalinawan were made of sturdy wood, propped high on stilts to stop wild animals from getting inside. Posts and doors were decorated with carvings of Great Bakunawa, the mother of all serpents and devourer of moons, who lived in the depths of the sea. The sight of the fearsome carvings sent a shiver down my back.

I reached my house, where a wooden figurine of my father, Datu Dakila, guarded the front door. He wielded a giant notched sword in one mighty fist, while around him coiled the powerful body of his air bakunawa, Buhawi.

Both he and Buhawi had bravely protected our village from a pack of vicious manananggal—flying ghouls with venom-tipped talons—but in the end, they had both succumbed to the creatures' poison.

My biggest dream was to become a great Serpent Rider like my father—fighting alongside my bakunawa to protect my home. Our village was built on the legends of our heroes, and I wanted people to tell stories about me too.

But without a bakunawa of my own, that dream was impossible.

I respectfully bowed before his statue. *I'm sorry I couldn't be like you.*

I had never truly known my father, since he died when I was a baby, yet I was always living in his shadow, trying to be the daughter I knew he would want me to be. But each day my bakunawa remained in its egg was a failure in my eyes.

I shook my head, clearing the dark thoughts away. *Your bakunawa* is *going to hatch, Tani. Everybody says so.*

I climbed the ladder into the main room, letting my eyes adjust to the dim interior. My bakunawa egg sat in a wooden cradle, infuriatingly still smooth and round. It was jet black, flecked with red and gold.

Picking up the egg, I turned it this way and that to check for even the tiniest hairline crack. As always, though, the surface beneath my fingers remained unbroken.

I set the egg down with a sigh. Some children tried using their swords to cleave their eggs in two, but bakunawa shells were harder than stone and were unbreakable to all but the creature itself. Still, my fingers itched with impatience.

"Please," I whispered. "Please hatch."

I prayed that the tiny creature inside the egg could hear me.

A faint, lilting melody filtered into the room. I padded over to the source—my younger sister's room.

I gently pushed aside the drapes to see Ligaya sitting by her window, working deftly at her loom as she hummed. Her eyes flickered to the doorway, then lit up as she saw me.

"Tani!" She ran over and gave me a fierce hug. Three white butterflies that had been perched on her lap fluttered away at the sudden disturbance. For some reason, wild creatures were always hanging around Ligaya. "Is training finished already?"

I grimaced, choosing not to answer.

"Oh! You're hurt." Ligaya pointed at some purpling bruises along my arms that I hadn't noticed until now. "Let me patch you up."

I sat down obediently as my sister bustled around her room, collecting jars of healing ointments.

"Where's Mother?" I asked as Ligaya smeared the cream on my arms.

Ligaya shrugged. "Probably away helping someone or other with this or that. Not that I'm complaining."

I couldn't help but grin at her nerve. Ligaya shouldn't have been speaking about our mother like that, but I knew what she meant. After my father died, the responsibility of leading the village came crashing down on our mother, Datu Eeya. That meant Ligaya and I weren't her only concern— every single person in the village was under her care. Mother was barely ever home. Instead of her, it was Ligaya who made me snacks to eat at training and patched me up after sparring. In turn, I helped Ligaya memorize tricky passages in her poems or fetched string for her weaving whenever she ran out.

Ever since I could remember, Ligaya and I had only had each other. We weren't sisters by blood, but we cared about each other so much that we might as well have been.

I was born under the Warrior's Star, but Ligaya had been born beneath the Story Chanter's Star, a rare but precious omen. While my own birth star destined me to a life of battle, Ligaya's fated her to a far different life as the village princess and history keeper.

Instead of a shield and blade, Ligaya's tools were words and song. Under the tutelage of our maidservant, Dalisay—a gnarled old woman who'd been the village princess in the days of my grandfather—Ligaya studied the history of our people. She learned stories from the dawn of time, like the cataclysmic war between the sky and the sea that caused the creation of all the islands in the world. One day, she would tell the tale of how the first humans had been born from the heart of a shattered bamboo stem. She would sing the ballads of our greatest heroes, weave sagas of the sun, moon, stars, and mountains, and speak the story of every living creature that called this land their home. Maybe one day, Ligaya would tell stories about me.

But this destiny also meant that Ligaya had to be protected at all costs. Knowledge was a strange power, and in the wrong hands it could be deadlier than the sharpest sword. On the very day she was born, she was sent to live with my mother, where she could be protected from every danger imaginable. Not only was Ligaya kept in strict seclusion, away from hard work on the rice fields or hazards on the fighting grounds, but it was forbidden for anyone to see her except for myself, my mother, the village healer, and Dalisay.

It was her fate to be hidden away like a priceless jewel until she mastered every story word for word, note for note. Then she would be allowed into the village to perform the stories for our festivals and celebrations. But sometimes, I caught Ligaya peering out the tiny window of her room, curious about life beyond the walls of our home.

"There." Ligaya sat back, satisfied with her work. For a ten-year-old, she was surprisingly good at taking care of people. "Also, your bakunawa hasn't hatched yet. I've been watching it all day."

A part of me bristled, but it was impossible to be angry at my kindhearted little sister. Trying to change the subject,

I glanced around the room and caught sight of a beautiful feather woven into the fabric that Ligaya was working on.

The feather was as long as my arm and gleamed with myriad colors when the moonlight hit it. I'd never seen anything like it before.

"Where'd you get this from?" I asked.

"A friend gave it to me," Ligaya replied, but didn't say anything more.

I smiled. "Well, this fabric is very nice. You're getting better."

"Thanks, but I'm sick of weaving. And making necklaces. And reciting stories."

I jerked a thumb in the direction of my bakunawa egg in the next room. "Now you know exactly how I feel waiting for *that* to hatch."

Ligaya was quiet for a moment. Suddenly, she looked up sharply. "I just remembered I've got to go somewhere."

I pursed my lips, having already guessed where this was going. "And that *somewhere* is not in this house, is it?"

"Of *course* it isn't. Otherwise, it wouldn't be interesting, would it?" Ligaya rolled her eyes. "And I was reciting the same old story all morning—Dalisay made me repeat it from the beginning each time I made a mistake. If I don't get out of here soon, I think I'm going to explode."

My sister had a point—memorizing the stories of our people *was* a hard job, especially since the longer ballads took hours, if not days, to recite—but I figured I should at least try to be a responsible older sister. "Even if Mother's not here, Dalisay won't let you leave."

"Don't worry about her. Trust me, she's probably sleeping." As if on cue, a loud snore from the adjacent room rattled through the walls.

"Fair enough." I grinned. "All right, but I'm coming with you."

Ligaya raced away like a bolt of lightning. Instead of going down the main ladder where she'd be seen by passersby, my sister shimmied out the back window and dropped onto the ground below. I followed her, my blood tingling with anticipation.

Our house was at the edge of the village, so I let Ligaya climb onto my shoulders to get over the blockade wall before I scrambled over it myself. Despite the perils in the deeper parts of the forest, the area closest to the village was harmless, as people went there most days to collect firewood.

We crept through the leaves, Ligaya dressed in a finely made blouse and skirt, and me with my sword and warrior gear. As the sound of crashing waves grew louder, Ligaya scampered up a tumble of boulders until she was perched as high as the trees.

"Look," Ligaya said as I clambered up the rocks to sit beside her.

Beyond the forest, the open sea stretched out before us.

"Isn't it beautiful?" Ligaya said wistfully. "Like liquid sky."

The moonlight glimmering on the waves created a pale,

shimmering path across the water. The ocean *was* beautiful, but I saw it every day. To me, it wasn't *that* special.

Ligaya looked at me expectantly. I tried and failed to find the right words—my sister had always been better at using flowery language than me. "It's, well . . . the sea."

Ligaya deflated a little. Then her eyes brightened as she gazed across the waves. "I wonder what would happen if I sailed all the way to that line," she said, pointing to the horizon. "I wonder if I'd fall right off the edge of the world."

In that moment, I felt a spark of connection with my little sister. Even though we had vastly different paths laid out before us, both of us were trapped, wishing for things that we couldn't have.

"Maybe Great Bakunawa would catch you before you made it that far." I grinned. I meant it as a joke, but Ligaya suddenly grew serious.

Everyone knew the stories of Great Bakunawa—Ligaya most of all. Great Bakunawa was the legendary primordial Serpent who lived at the bottom of the ocean, stirring up currents and causing hurricanes, earthquakes, and tidal waves. In days of old, villagers had destroyed bakunawa eggs to prevent even more disasters from happening. At the same time, they also discovered that loud noises could scare the Serpent away.

But Great Bakunawa was most notorious for devouring the moons. Long ago, seven moons illuminated the night sky. Soon after people started fighting back against Great Bakunawa, the Serpent snapped up the first moon.

According to the stories, it was because she was so jealous of the moons' beauty that she couldn't help but have them for herself. Luckily, the Mahika—the strongest magician in the land—cast an enchantment on Great Bakunawa before she could swallow the other moons, banishing the Serpent to the bottom of the ocean.

But that peace wouldn't last. The Mahika warned that Great Bakunawa was too powerful to be imprisoned by magic forever. Every hundred years, Great Bakunawa could break free of the enchantment and return to swallow another moon.

The Mahika realized that the only way people could stand against the Moon Eater was if they had serpents of their own to fight with. So she convinced her people to tame the bakunawa hatchlings rather than destroy them. With elemental serpents on their side, they stood a chance of vanquishing Great Bakunawa when she came back.

Only those who the Spirits deemed worthy—those born beneath the Warrior's Star—could hatch and bond with bakunawa. Those warriors became the Serpent Riders, who formed the secret village of Kalinawan to hone their fighting skills.

Although the Serpent Riders trained hard and did their best to stop her, Great Bakunawa never failed to return every century and devour the next moon. Even the Mahika's power, which could control most creatures, could do nothing against the Serpent's rampage.

After Great Bakunawa swallowed the sixth moon,

leaving only one left in the sky, the Mahika suddenly disappeared. Without her power to maintain the balance of nature, monsters began to breed. They set their hungry sights on humans, forcing the warriors to fight back—but defeating these new enemies made the Serpent Riders stronger than ever.

The Serpent Riders always believed the Spirits would gift us a hero who would defeat Great Bakunawa once and for all. When my father became the greatest warrior Kalinawan had ever seen, everyone thought it would be *him* who would save our moon. When he was killed, his legacy fell to me— the daughter who was born on the day he died.

Our moon's last hope rested on me. If I didn't stop Great Bakunawa when she broke free of the enchantment, the final moon would be devoured, and the night sky would plunge into eternal darkness.

"Great Bakunawa is exactly why I came here," Ligaya said. "I dreamed about her last night."

Ligaya looked out over the glittering waves as if she could almost see the mighty Serpent breaking the surface of the water, the moon disappearing into her cavernous maw. A frightful image for sure, but hadn't Ligaya just said it was only a dream?

I gave an exasperated sigh. "You *always* have nightmares about Great Bakunawa, and every time the moon stays hanging in the sky. Your stories are making you scared of the shadows. If I'd known this was why you wanted to see the ocean, I'd never have let you come here."

Ligaya gazed at the sky. "But what will we do when she comes back? The stories say that the only way to stop the Serpent from devouring the moon is to give her a sacrifice that can stand in the moon's place. A sacrifice just as pure, just as beautiful."

For some reason, my sister's words made me shiver. "Well, the stories also say that Great Bakunawa *can't* come back until the Mahika's hundred-year enchantment is up. And that won't happen for many years—not before I become a warrior."

Ligaya frowned. "When the Spirits choose the Mahika, they grant the power to control nature, on the condition that the power is used to protect all living creatures. She couldn't have just abandoned us, so she must still be missing. Can the Mahika's enchantment really hold Great Bakunawa captive if she's gone?"

Ligaya's words made sense. But it was hard to take her worry seriously when I knew we weren't in any danger right now.

"For all her light, the moon was captive, held behind a cage of teeth," Ligaya murmured, reciting the first lines of the familiar epic. "In the stories, the moon-eating Serpent has an insatiable appetite. Perhaps Great Bakunawa is still hungry . . . perhaps she's just waiting for the perfect time."

This was going way too far for my liking. Looking at my sister sternly, I pointed to the sea. "Do you *see* Great Bakunawa swimming through the water, coming back to eat our moon?"

"No . . ."

"Then we have nothing to worry about. Great Bakunawa *isn't* coming back anytime soon. Promise me you won't terrify yourself anymore, all right?"

Ligaya gave a hesitant nod.

"And when Great Bakunawa *does* come back—well, I'll have my own bakunawa and I'll be a great Serpent Rider. Remember, *I'm* going to protect our moon. I'm going to protect *you*." I grinned.

Ligaya cracked a small smile in return. Not knowing what else to say, I glanced back at the village. A plume of dark smoke billowed from one of the houses, but it wasn't on fire. In fact, it was a common enough sight that no one paid much attention to it.

That house belonged to Babaylan Kalan-ya, our healer who could connect the mortal world with that of the Spirits. People asked the babaylan for anything from special medicine to predicting how next year's harvest would go. The magical smoke allowed her to see things that the rest of us couldn't. Twelve years ago, the old woman foresaw Great Bakunawa's return to devour the last moon—and that Tanikala the Serpent Rider, daughter of Datu Dakila, would defeat the Moon Eater for good.

Everyone in the village knew that prophecy. Still, a tiny voice in my mind asked, *How are you going to fight Great Bakunawa when you don't even have your own serpent?*

I gazed at the smoke, thinking I could see strange shapes twisting in the cloud. Suddenly, I had an idea.

"Tani?" asked Ligaya. "Is something wrong?"

"It's nothing," I mumbled, even as a plan began to form in my mind. "We've been out here long enough. It's time to go home."

Chapter 2

The next morning, I walked quickly through the village, passing people carrying bundles of firewood, baskets of vegetables, or jars of water. I dodged through the flurry, knowing exactly where I was heading—to Babaylan Kalan-ya's house.

If anyone knew what was happening with my bakunawa, it was her.

Because of the nature of her work, her house wasn't built on stilts, and instead sat right on the ground. I rang the chime outside the door before pushing through the curtains.

Inside, the air was thick with the pungent smell of a thousand different herbs and ingredients. Pots of tinctures and metal instruments were arranged neatly on the floor. The babaylan crouched over a firepit, her head encased in the hazy smoke that filled the entire room and drifted out a hole in the ceiling.

I waited patiently until Babaylan Kalan-ya was done with her seeing. Finally, she sat back, then glanced at me with eyes surrounded by wrinkles, like she'd known I was standing there this whole time.

"Tanikala," she said, her voice as creaky as old floorboards. "What brings you to visit this poorly old woman?"

I didn't waste any time. "My bakunawa egg," I told her. "When will it hatch?"

The babaylan chuckled, looking to the side like she could see someone who wasn't there. "Impatient as always, just like her father." She turned back to me. "Some things you cannot rush. It would break the natural order—like if a child grew up before their time, they wouldn't be ready for what was expected of them."

"But it's been so *long*," I complained. "Bato's egg hatched two years ago, and almost everyone else has their bakunawa as well. *I* was born to defeat Great Bakunawa, so why does mine have to be the last?"

"Perhaps you're looking at it the wrong way," Babaylan Kalan-ya countered. "The Moon Eater won't return for many years. Your bakunawa is building its strength for the day it will finally have to face its mother. Perhaps it's just waiting for the right time . . . just like you must learn to do."

I bit back a frustrated sigh. "Well, could you look into the smoke anyway?"

"I am old, and the seeing-smoke takes a toll on my body. Use it too much, and there are . . . consequences." Her eyes darkened.

Just then, the chime outside gave a frantic ring before a panic-stricken man poked his head through the door. "Babaylan, please come quickly! Hiraya's child is being born."

Moving fast, the old woman gathered a basket of tools and supplies. "I am sorry, Tanikala. But you will learn that wisdom rewards the patient."

The babaylan swept through the door and was gone.

I slumped against the wall. If only my bakunawa egg had hatched already—then I wouldn't have wasted my time coming here.

My nose itched with the smell of the seeing-smoke. Babaylan Kalan-ya hadn't put out the coals—wasn't she worried her house would catch fire? *Maybe I should put it out for her . . .*

I crouched beside the firepit, watching the smoke swirl into the air.

Can this really make you see the future?

Another darker idea wormed into my mind.

I glanced furtively around to make sure nobody was watching. I was no babaylan, but surely if I made my request very clear, the Spirits would understand.

Closing my eyes, I leaned over the smoke. I repeated a single thought over and over in time with my heartbeat. *I want a bakunawa. I want a bakunawa.*

I breathed, feeling the smoke settle in my body. The tips of my fingers tingled, then my arms, then my chest. My surroundings faded away, replaced by gnarled trees that towered around me.

I know where I am. The forest.

I was in a waking dream. I was still aware of my real body crouched over the smoldering coals, but in my mind's eye, another Tani walked through the forest, picking out a path through the dense foliage.

Eventually, the trees opened into a small clearing where a figure bent over a campfire, stirring an iron pot.

My dream-self drew closer. The woman, who was about the same age as my mother, looked up and stared right at me like she knew I was there.

"Would you like some food, traveler?" she asked with a kind smile.

Instinctively, I shook my head.

"Then why have you come to visit me?"

I hesitated, unsure why the vision had brought me to this strange woman. But since Babaylan Kalan-ya's seeings were rarely wrong, I decided to trust the process.

"I need a bakunawa. I need to be a warrior like my father so I can save the moon."

The woman looked amused, like she'd known that would be my answer. "I can certainly help you with that, though you will have to come to me yourself."

So she wanted me to visit her in real life rather than in this vision. I was dubious. She didn't look like a warrior. "How can you help me?"

"A wandering woman like me has many . . . talents. Just moments ago, I was in a land far away from here, and then I heard you call me through the smoke. So, I came." Her smile broadened. "That isn't the only magic trick I know. It will be easy enough for me to craft a bakunawa to your liking."

"*Craft* one?" I couldn't help but sound incredulous. "You can't spin a bakunawa out of thin air. I just hoped you could make my egg hatch."

The woman waved her hand dismissively. "Speeding up that natural process would take a lot of time, effort, and concentration. Trust me, this method is far more efficient."

I decided to give her a chance. "What do I need to do?"

"When you come to me, you must bring three things: a handful of charcoal, a walis tingting, and a blue cone shell," she instructed as if reciting a recipe.

Two of those were easy enough to find. Charcoal could be taken from a fire, and a walis tingting was a palm-leaf broom that everyone cleaned their houses with.

The only ingredient that would be some trouble was the blue cone shell. As far as I knew, only one such shell existed— and it sat right on Babaylan Kalan-ya's windowsill.

My eyes narrowed. "This had better not be a trick."

"Oh, of course not," the woman replied airily. "Think of it as a transaction."

Despite her reassurances, a part of me was still uneasy. This woman—if she even existed—was far too mysterious to risk meeting in the dead of night.

I wouldn't be taking her up on her offer.

"Thank you," I said anyway, since my mother taught me to be polite. "I never found out your name."

The woman smiled again. "You can call me Mutya."

☽

The vision dissipated as I leaned away from the pungent smoke to breathe in fresher air. Luckily, the babaylan's house was still empty except for me.

That was close. As I hurried home, I couldn't even begin to imagine how much trouble I'd be in if I was caught doing a seeing on my own. And I still didn't have any answers as to why my bakunawa was taking so long to emerge.

Maybe Babaylan Kalan-ya was right. Maybe there is *no answer except waiting for the egg to hatch in its own time.* Still, each day that passed without my bakunawa made me bubble with impatience—like a persistent itch I couldn't scratch.

Loud cheers made me look up. A crowd was gathered outside a house, chatting excitedly.

I blinked. That was *Kiri's* house.

Not caring about niceties, I shouldered my way through the press of people. My small friend sat on the ground with a huge smile plastered across his face.

Coiled around his shoulders was a sea-green bakunawa.

My jaw dropped open.

"Tani!" Kiri flung himself forward and wrapped his arms tight around me. "He hatched! I can't believe it!"

Me neither, I thought, feeling faint. "When?"

"I don't really know," said Kiri, his face flushed in excitement. "I woke up and he was already here, waiting for me."

The bakunawa nuzzled his scaly head against Kiri's neck, making my friend laugh.

I studied the serpent curiously. "He's definitely a water bakunawa. What did you name him?"

"You know, I always worried about what I would call my bakunawa when it hatched. But as soon as I saw him, his name just popped into my head." Kiri grinned. "It's Luntian. Doesn't it suit him?"

"That's a great name." I forced a smile.

Kiri's mother bustled through the crowd, tears sparkling in her eyes as she announced, "Tonight we'll hold a special feast for Kiri and Luntian. All are invited!"

Everyone cheered. Kalinawan was such a tight-knit community that the entire village was automatically invited whenever there was a party, but hatchling celebrations were especially extravagant, almost like a new human child had been born. There was even a special tradition where the bakunawa's eggshells were thrown back into the sea as a last tribute to Great Bakunawa, the serpents' mother. Despite the ravages Great Bakunawa had wreaked upon our world, we still owed her respect for the fact that her children were the reason we could protect ourselves from monsters—or at least that was what Swordmaster Pai taught us. It was a great honor for a warrior to train alongside a bakunawa, and we gave each hatchling the celebration it deserved.

"I can't wait to celebrate with you, Tani! And we'll get to eat my mother's famous ube halaya," Kiri said.

I *wanted* to be happy for my friend—having a bakunawa was all we'd ever dreamed of—but the thought of celebrating someone else's bakunawa when I was so desperately hoping for mine made me feel utterly miserable.

Nobody but me was meant to protect our moon. Now *everyone* but me had a bakunawa. I could almost hear Bato saying those exact words in a mocking voice.

"Yeah," I said, my stomach sinking. "I'll try to come."

Kiri was so caught up in his excitement that he didn't even notice me leave.

When I returned home, my bakunawa egg lay still and silent in its cradle, as stubborn as ever.

It's just waiting for the right time, Babaylan Kalan-ya had said.

But now, it felt like that day would never come.

Chapter 3

Hours later, I sat on the rocks overlooking the shoreline, sharpening my father's sword. I ran the whetstone up and down the blade in a thoughtless, mechanical motion. Taking care of our weapons was a lesson that Swordmaster Pai had drilled into us from the beginning, but it was also a task that comforted me whenever something was weighing on my mind.

I could see all the way down to the beach where Kiri and Luntian's party was in full swing. A giant bonfire shot sparks high into the night, and the summer breeze carried the mouthwatering smell of roasted food. I could barely hear the rasping of the whetstone over the noise of the music and merrymaking.

My blade was already as sharp as a bakunawa's talons, but for an aspiring Serpent Rider like me, it could never be sharp enough.

Reaching into my sash, I pulled out my bakunawa egg. I'd hardly taken my eyes off it since finding out about Kiri's serpent—secretly hoping that, just maybe, today would be the day. But the egg remained unbroken, its red and gold flecks glinting weakly in the moonlight.

My father's bakunawa had hatched when he was only six years old. According to Babaylan Kalan-ya, it was the earliest bakunawa hatching in the Serpent Riders' history. Now I was twice that age and still had no serpent.

I was the daughter of our greatest warrior, the one destined to save our moon—but how was I supposed to do that when I didn't even have a bakunawa?

The sound of my frustrated sigh skittered over the silent rocks.

Suddenly, I heard stone scraping, a muffled footstep. My hand dropped instinctively to my sword.

Someone's here.

Then a familiar face peeked above the rocks.

I rolled my eyes. "You're not supposed to be here, Ligaya."

Ligaya laughed as I helped her scramble up the last few boulders. "Come on, there's a party! There's no way I couldn't sneak out. Actually, I was hoping you'd get me some food, but seeing as you're sitting here . . ."

My sister wore a dark cloak with a deep hood hiding her face. Even with the party going on, she wouldn't risk being discovered.

Ligaya plopped down beside me onto a patch of

shrubbery. That kind of plant would be dotted with yellow flowers during the day, but now the buds were closed against the chill of the night.

"What *are* you doing here anyway?" she asked with a sideways glance. "Shouldn't you be down there celebrating? I can't believe Kiri has a bakunawa now. Isn't that . . ."

Ligaya trailed off as she noticed my dark expression. Her gaze fell to the bakunawa egg in my lap.

"I don't know why it's taking so long," I said, biting back my anger.

Wordlessly, Ligaya reached for the egg. I handed it over and she weighed it in her hands.

"I don't know, Tani," she said. "Yours feels . . . different."

"How?" I felt a flash of indignation at her matter-of-fact tone. "Is something wrong with it?"

Ligaya shrugged, frowning. "I'm not sure how to explain. Sometimes Babaylan Kalan-ya lets me hold the new eggs after she harvests them from Great Bakunawa's sacred pool. When I hold them, I feel something . . . like a thrum, a pulse." She looked at me. "With yours, there's nothing. Maybe it's sick?"

Sick? The thought had never even occurred to me before. But my sister *was* a storyteller—perhaps she knew more about bakunawa hatchlings than I did. Although, I didn't know how she could claim to *feel* that something was different about my bakunawa.

More roughly than I intended, I snatched the egg out of Ligaya's grasp. I already knew that I was going to become a

30

great warrior—it was unthinkable, impossible even, for my bakunawa to have any weakness at all.

"It will be fine," I said, forcing myself to believe my own words. "It's just taking its time."

Instead of replying, Ligaya glanced at Datu Dakila's kampilan, still lying across my lap. The weapon had a heavy notched blade and a wooden hilt carved into the likeness of a bakunawa's head. There were many, many stories that had been told about this sword—and one day, Ligaya would know them all.

My sister's voice rose in a soft melody. *"Shadows could do nothing but before this blade to fall . . ."*

I knew that song. It was the story of how this kampilan was passed down to the warriors in my family ever since Great Bakunawa first stormed the seas, of how my ancestors wielded the sword to vanquish monsters and protect our people.

Just like the heart of a true warrior, this blade had been tested in countless battles, reforged in the heat of a hundred fires—but its tempered core remained pure, strong, and unyielding.

My sister gave a small smile as she finished the verse. "You know, Tani, if it wasn't for your bakunawa, I'd have thought you were a Serpent Rider already. You're the bravest person I've ever met."

I blinked at the unexpected praise. The words would have been empty flattery from some, but I knew my sister, and Ligaya always told the truth as she saw it. I was torn between wanting to snap at her for continuing to remind me of my bakunawa's silence and wrapping her in the biggest hug I could give.

If I was brave when I carried this sword, it wasn't because of anything I'd done. It was because of who had borne this blade before, whose hands and spirits guided me when I wielded it. Without a bakunawa of my own, how could I ever prove myself worthy?

But then I remembered this kampilan was never given to just anybody. It was always the weapon of great heroes—and if it was now mine, surely that meant I would be a great hero too. I just needed to believe it.

"Maybe," I said. "But there's no way I can be a Serpent Rider if I don't have an actual serpent."

Ligaya had no response to that. When I looked up from my sword, I saw that she'd pulled stems from the shrubbery around her and braided them into a little wreath. I wasn't surprised, considering all the weaving she did at home. But what really astonished me was that the stalks in Ligaya's hands were blooming with yellow flowers—the same flowers that were sealed just minutes before.

"How did you do that?" I asked. The rest of the shrubs around Ligaya remained devoid of color, as they would until morning. Even in the dim moonlight, the petals in her hands were as bright as the summer sun.

"They were sleeping," she mumbled, shrugging. "I just asked them to wake up."

"Asked them to . . ." *Is she talking about the flowers?* At a loss for words, I pointed at the wreath she'd made. "That's far too small for you, isn't it?"

"I'm not making it for me." Her eyes flickered past me. I followed her gaze to the nearby treetops, where I spotted a small, winged creature and the slightest glimmer of rainbow feathers. I blinked, then whatever I had seen vanished in a rustle of leaves.

"Is that the *friend* you were talking about earlier?" I asked, remembering the iridescent feather in Ligaya's room.

My sister nodded but said nothing. I shook my head. First the white butterflies, now whatever that creature was.

"Next thing you know," I said with a smile, "you'll be calling Great Bakunawa to our doorstep."

Ligaya laughed. The sound was still ringing in the air when a shout tore through the night.

It was followed by another, louder and shriller than the one before. The lively drums and gongs from Kiri and Luntian's party abruptly fell quiet.

I got to my feet, heart pounding. People cried out in panic. Although their voices were muffled by the distance, I heard one word repeated over and over.

Swordmaster Pai's commanding voice cut through the chaos, cracking through the night like thunder. "Berberoka! Berberoka! Serpent Riders, to arms!"

It can't be. There hadn't been a monster attack this close to the village since my father met his end in battle.

My gaze locked with Ligaya's, my own shock and fear mirrored in her eyes. As the story keeper, she knew more about berberoka than I did—no doubt her imagination was conjuring up all sorts of horrors.

"We're going home," I said. "Now."

Face pale, Ligaya rolled up the hem of her dress and tied it around her knees so she could run. After draping her cloak around her shoulders and pulling up the hood, she became just another shadow in the dark.

I nodded in approval. My sister really *had* mastered the art of secrecy—everyone else would be too preoccupied with running for their lives to notice that the veiled princess was out of doors.

We dashed down the rocks as quickly as we dared and sprinted back to the village. Already, a few terrified party-goers had made it behind the walls, their fine clothes and jewelry in disarray.

I placed my bakunawa egg in Ligaya's hands. "Take this and go to your room. Don't come out until it's safe."

Ligaya's eyes were wide. "What are you going to do?"

"Live up to my destiny," I replied. "I'm going to be a warrior."

Before I could lose my nerve, I slung my sash and sword over my shoulder and ran toward the beach.

Chapter 4

I staggered as a huge tremor shook the earth, vibrations buzzing through my bones.

Frightened people shoved past me, running back to the safety of the walls. Many shot bewildered glances my way when they noticed I was heading *toward* the danger instead of away from it. The sight of everyone fleeing made me hesitate, but only for a moment. Fighting monsters was what I'd trained for all my life. I knew what I had to do.

And if a berberoka really *was* attacking our village, then flimsy wooden walls wouldn't do much to protect the villagers anyway.

The packed earth turned to sand beneath my feet as I reached the shore. Kiri was having his party on our practice field and his family had set up tables laden with food. Now plates of rice, steamed vegetables, and roasted meat lay strewn across the sand, scattered in the chaos.

Two dozen Serpent Riders remained gathered around Swordmaster Pai, facing the threat head-on.

Only then did I look at the creature that had sent almost everyone fleeing for their lives.

The berberoka finally plodded out of the sea. Clumps of algae and lichen clung to its stonelike body, obscuring a thick brow that jutted over squinting eyes. It was as if an ancient boulder had dislodged from the sea floor and had come to wreak havoc on our village. I thought the monsters in Ligaya's tales were almost too fantastical to believe, but in the shifting light of the bonfire, the beast looked even more impossible than anything the stories told me to imagine.

Kiri, Bato, and the other warrior novices stood among the Serpent Riders facing the berberoka. Kiri looked like a ghost, and I suspected he would have run far away if he hadn't been frozen in fear. Even Bato wasn't wearing his usual arrogant smile.

"You didn't say you were inviting a berberoka to your party," I said to Kiri as I reached him.

My friend stared helplessly back. The jibe had probably sailed completely over his head. Beside him, Luntian's emerald scales were pale with fear. We all flinched as the berberoka roared, sending salt water spraying into our faces.

"Happy birthday," I told Luntian weakly.

A voice shouted in our direction, "Novices! Get out of here!"

Though he was talking to us, Swordmaster Pai never took his eyes off the berberoka, his face as fierce as a summer storm. He looked formidable in his serpent-scale armor, the sharp blade of his war golok reflecting the moonlight. His sword wasn't like any other I'd seen—instead of tapering to a point, the blade widened out to form a flat wedge. I had no doubt that in our teacher's hands, the heavy sword could chop off the berberoka's arm in one strike.

"Help the villagers get to safety," Swordmaster Pai commanded.

The berberoka trudged up the beach, each leg the size of a tree trunk. Algae dripped off its fingers and trailed along the sand. Now that it was out of the water, the creature looked impossibly huge—even Swordmaster Pai was dwarfed by its might.

"Safety?" I said incredulously. "That thing would flatten Kalinawan just by stomping on it."

My teacher let out a strained laugh. His disdain was evident as he said, "Supposedly Babaylan Kalan-ya has a magical charm that protects the village from monsters. I don't think *anything* can stop the berberoka, but getting everyone behind the walls is our best and only hope." He gave me a stern look. "Now, all of you, go!"

Not wanting to disobey a direct order, Bato, Kiri, and I ran toward the remaining villagers. With the other novices, we helped those who couldn't get away quickly enough, or those too terrified to move. But as the berberoka let out another earthshaking roar that sounded like waves crashing, I couldn't help but glance back to watch the fight.

The Serpent Riders warily circled the berberoka. Without

37

breaking stride, the sea-ogre swung its arm in a deadly arc, forcing warriors to jump out of the way. The berberoka's fingers plowed into the ground, scoring deep slashes in the sand.

One of the Serpent Riders leaped onto the back of his bakunawa, its scales the color of sapphire. The water bakunawa shot into the sky—far from the berberoka's reach.

"Ice!" the Serpent Rider commanded.

Around the bakunawa, a dozen glittering shards of ice crystallized from the air, each the length of my arm. One after another, the ice shards streaked down and thudded into the berberoka's body. But although the shards were dagger-sharp, they couldn't pierce through the sea-ogre's rocky hide. The berberoka swept its hand across its body and shattered all the ice shards into frozen dust.

As the Serpent Rider circled back, trying to aim another strike, the berberoka picked up a massive piece of driftwood like it was a twig. Nearby warriors hurriedly stepped away, knowing that one sweep of the wooden club would shatter all their bones.

But the berberoka wasn't aiming for them. The ogre pulled its arm back, squinting at the sky.

I gasped. "Watch out!"

Even if the warrior heard my warning, it came too late. The berberoka hurled the branch into the sky with the strength of ten men. The Serpent Rider in the air barely had time to pull away before the driftwood slammed into his bakunawa, tangling its coils like a trap.

Rider and serpent tumbled out of the sky, landing hard in a broken heap.

My teeth ground together as I bit back a scream. The remaining Serpent Riders were momentarily stunned, staring at their fallen comrade.

Only one thought was clear through the chaos. One mistake, one wrong move, and it would all be over.

Without warning, Bato turned and started sprinting back toward the shoreline. Iska bolted after him in a streak of copper.

"What are you *doing*?" I shouted in disbelief. I knew he wasn't the sharpest of us novices, but this was too far, even for him.

Bato glared at me over his shoulder like I was the one being ridiculous. "Did you even see what just happened? We can't just stand here and do nothing!"

He drew both his swords and charged for the berberoka.

I blinked after him in shock. I couldn't believe he was joining a battle he knew he couldn't possibly win. And yet . . .

How could I ever hope to call myself a Serpent Rider, to defeat Great Bakunawa, if I ran away at my first real fight? This was my chance to show my worth as a warrior.

Besides, I'd never forgive myself if I let Bato prove he was braver than me.

"Keep the others safe!" I shouted at Kiri before running after Bato. This was either the most courageous or the most reckless thing I'd ever done in my life.

Though the Serpent Riders fought valiantly, none of their

blades could break through the berberoka's rocklike skin. Even the bakunawa's elemental attacks didn't harm the monster so much as make it even more furious.

The berberoka crushed its fist around a Serpent Rider who hadn't gotten away quickly enough. Its other fist slammed into the warrior's bakunawa, sending it spinning along the sand.

I flinched in horror. This was *not* going well.

Suddenly, my gaze locked with Swordmaster Pai's. His eyes widened at the sight of me.

"Get back!" he shouted.

But I couldn't move. All I could see was the berberoka's rocky fist punching into the Serpent Rider's frail body. I wanted nothing more than to heed Swordmaster Pai and run—yet I had known these people all my life. I couldn't just leave them to their fate.

I quickly glanced back to see if everyone had made it behind the walls, but what I saw made me stop short.

Someone was sprinting *in the wrong direction*—away from the protection of the walls, across the sand toward us. Toward the berberoka that had finished off two Serpent Riders like they were nothing but playthings to be thrown away. The figure was small and slight, wearing a hooded cloak.

"Kiri?" I breathed incredulously. My friend couldn't even make it through training on some days. I couldn't believe that he was willingly returning to a battle against a living monster.

But the running figure didn't have a sea-green bakunawa trailing behind it. The dark hood blew back, and illuminated by the bonfire, the person's face was set in fearful determination.

I gasped.

It wasn't Kiri. It was Ligaya.

I didn't realize I was running toward her until we almost crashed together. Stunned, I grasped my sister's hands, feeling her small ones tremble in mine. A thousand questions pounded through my head. *What are you doing here? Why didn't you stay at home? Why didn't you listen to me?*

None of those thoughts made it past my lips. "Run," was all I managed. "As fast as you can."

Ligaya's eyes became blank pools of fear as she finally understood the danger.

Not long ago, Ligaya had complained about having to memorize stories about warriors and monsters. Now a real battle was playing out . . . and she'd flung herself right into the middle of it.

Ligaya whispered, "I . . . I know what you have to do."

It took a few moments for her meaning to sink in. Ligaya knew all the stories better than any of us. I didn't want her to be here, but right now—facing a foe impossible to defeat—I realized she was our only chance.

"You can't attack it through its skin," Ligaya said breathlessly. "In the stories, the heroes always strike the only place where the berberoka's armor doesn't protect it. Aim for its eyes."

I nodded sharply. I released my sister's hands, hating myself for leaving her, though I didn't have a choice. "Thank you, Ligaya. Now *go*."

Pulling up her hood, Ligaya dashed back toward the village. I hoped with everything I had that she would make it back to safety.

Suddenly, my legs almost gave way as the ground rocked wildly. The berberoka had come closer—too close.

I whirled, bringing my sword to bear as the berberoka's shadow fell over me. I stared into the rutted crags that formed its face, imagining the small black orbs that peered from beneath its rocky brow. *Aim for its eyes . . .*

But the berberoka wasn't coming for me. I leaped out of the way as it trudged forward, paying no heed to the elemental strikes from the bakunawa. The ogre let out a grating roar, lifting its hand to attack . . .

I blinked. There were no Serpent Riders that far up the beach.

And then a scream pierced the night. Horror spiked through me. I recognized the voice.

The berberoka targeted the one person who was completely defenseless. The only one with no weapon and no bakunawa.

Ligaya.

My sister scrambled backward and fell hard onto the sand, her mouth open in terror.

Move! my mind cried, but my feet wouldn't obey. My fingers were paralyzed and my sword was suddenly heavy as stone. But even if I could have run, I wouldn't have been fast enough to help Ligaya. If I had a bakunawa, it could have seized Ligaya in its coils and whisked her out of the berberoka's path.

But I didn't have a bakunawa. I only had myself—Tani, the failed warrior, who could do *nothing* to save her sister in time . . .

"Iska!" Bato yelled behind me. "Fire!"

A stream of flames blazed past me, hot enough to rival the bonfire that still burned on the sand. Fire licked up the berberoka's legs as Bato's copper bakunawa unleashed the full force of her power.

Leaving my sister in the sand, the monster swung back around to face the new threat, its swaying arms narrowly missing Ligaya. Although the heat was fierce, the flames died down to reveal that the sea-ogre was charred but unharmed. As the sparks faded around Iska's jaws, the berberoka glowered down at Bato.

Bato stared back at the monster in frozen disbelief. The berberoka lifted one mighty foot, ready to squash him like an insect.

Swordmaster Pai dived across the sand in a running leap, tackling Bato out of the way, just as the berberoka's foot crashed down onto the ground where Bato had stood just moments before.

"Didn't I tell you to go?" Swordmaster Pai roared.

Shaken, Bato staggered to his feet. Ligaya stumbled the last few paces to the village and slipped back behind the gate.

"Its eyes," I yelled frantically at Swordmaster Pai. "We have to aim for its eyes!"

But how could we hold out against something that big? With the berberoka's swinging arms, we'd never get close enough to strike its eyes.

The monster continued its relentless march, an unstoppable force of nature. As we watched helplessly, it reached the first house and raised both fists, ready to crash them down onto the terrified people inside.

"No!" I shouted.

As the berberoka's fists swung down, something strange happened. Instead of crushing the house like kindling, the berberoka hit an invisible barrier, its powerful strike coming to a stop just above the house's roof. The berberoka tried to smash again and again to no avail.

This is magic. I couldn't believe the enchantment had always surrounded our village and I hadn't seen it in action until now.

Still, the barrier couldn't hold forever. Already I saw thin translucent cracks spreading through the air like spiderwebs.

We were running out of time.

"If only there was a way to hold it down," Swordmaster Pai muttered.

The berberoka shuffled as it tried and failed to breach Babaylan Kalan-ya's magical barrier. This far up the beach, the sand was drier and lighter, dragging the berberoka down.

The idea came to me in a flash. *That's it.*

"Swordmaster," I said. "Look at the sand. If we use the earth bakunawa's magic, maybe we can . . ."

My teacher grinned in understanding. "Tani, that's a fantastic idea." He drew a deep breath. "Earth bakunawa, to me!"

Seven Serpent Riders rallied to the swordmaster, their bakunawa the colors of granite, ochre, and deep soil. It didn't take long for the warriors to catch on to the plan. I felt a pulsing beneath my feet as the bakunawa's magic seeped into the sand, calling the earth to awaken.

Black sand swarmed up the berberoka's feet like each tiny grain was alive. At first, the sea-ogre shook off the sand in irritation, but as the magic grew, sand crawled up its ankles, its knees, trapping it as surely as iron shackles.

The berberoka stumbled, reaching out a hand to steady itself. But no sooner had its stony fingers touched the sand than its entire hand was sucked into an inescapable pit. The monster howled in rage and desperation—knowing it was impossible to fight against the earth itself.

Here's our chance.

"Together," Swordmaster Pai shouted. "Now!"

As one, the Serpent Riders charged at the berberoka with a fearsome battle cry. The berberoka lashed out wildly with its free arm, striking one of the warriors and sending her flying down the beach.

Swordmaster Pai had been quick enough to duck beneath the blow. As the rest of us distracted the berberoka with our flashing blades, he scrambled up the berberoka's body like he was scaling a cliff face, until he stood precariously on the monster's shoulder. The berberoka shook itself angrily, but the old swordmaster held on.

"Be careful!" I yelled as the berberoka reached up, its fingers set like claws.

Swordmaster Pai wasted no time. With a bloodcurdling shout, he swung his war golok up and around—straight into the berberoka's beady black eye.

The berberoka roared as the sharpened iron dug in deep. It tried to swipe at the swordmaster again, but the veteran had already leaped away, rolling as he hit the sand. The berberoka clawed at the sword still lodged in its eye, but between its stubby fingers and jutting brow, the sword was like a tiny splinter impossible to pull out.

"Run!" my teacher cried, grabbing my arm.

A low, rumbling sound erupted from the berberoka, like stone sliding against stone. The berberoka's upraised hand disintegrated into smaller rocks as the force that bound them together gave way.

I sprang aside as the berberoka's legs collapsed. A loud *thump* resounded behind me as the ogre's torso hit the sand, then a series of smaller *clacks* as the rest of its body clattered on top. When I turned back, nothing remained of the monster except a pile of ordinary-looking boulders.

I stopped running to catch my breath. After the chaos, the silence was jarring.

Every muscle inside me was driven to exhaustion. The

warriors exchanged grim glances. Even Bato looked uncharacteristically solemn. I couldn't believe we'd faced down a berberoka and were still breathing.

But I already knew that not all of us had been so lucky.

Tonight began as a celebration, but it couldn't have ended more differently. We'd defeated a monster straight out of Ligaya's stories, but three brave Serpent Riders were now gone forever.

Chapter 5

From on high, the lonely moon watched as I crept through the village. It was the night after the berberoka attack, and most of the villagers were already asleep, exhausted after a long day of cleaning up its aftermath. Even our warrior training had been put on hold as we paid respects to the Serpent Riders lost in the battle.

I couldn't stop thinking about the attack and how helpless I felt. *Would I have been more useful if I had a bakunawa, if I could have helped the other Serpent Riders?* After many long and tiring hours arguing with myself, I knew without a doubt what I had to do.

Silent as a ghost, I made my way to the beach. I half expected to see Swordmaster Pai there, keeping vigil for the fallen warriors as he had all through the previous night. But I was alone, my only companions the waves whispering against the shore.

I crouched beside the remains of the bonfire from Kiri's

party and poured a handful of cooled charcoal into a jar. There was already a walis tingting clutched under my arm, taken from Dalisay's room—that woman slept so deeply, she'd be oblivious even if a horde of kapre giants tore the roof off the walls.

Now for the shell.

I snuck between the houses until I reached Babaylan Kalan-ya's home. The blue cone shell sat on the windowsill in the same spot I'd always seen it in. I felt a pang of doubt and guilt—Babaylan Kalan-ya was like a grandmother to me. Stealing from her was the worst betrayal.

It's been sitting here collecting dust for years, I told myself. *Surely she won't even notice if it goes missing.*

Before I could lose my nerve, I tucked the fist-sized shell into my sash, completing the list of items. The only thing left to do now was to meet Mutya.

And that will be the hardest part.

The sand dragged at my feet as I trudged up the beach to the edge of the forest. The sea behind me whispered, calling me home.

I clenched my fists. If I turned back, I'd still be the last novice without a bakunawa. I'd be just as helpless as the night before. It didn't matter how fast I could run, how quickly I could dodge, or how skilled I was with my sword. The berberoka had shown me there was no way I could ever protect Kalinawan—protect Ligaya—if I didn't have a bakunawa.

Besides, I wouldn't be completely defenseless against

Mutya. Kiri and Ligaya were right—aside from my unhatched egg, I was the best fighter among the novices.

I touched the hilt of the kampilan across my back. This was my father's sword; the sword that had slain monsters. And if the wandering woman tried anything suspicious, she would find herself coming face-to-face with a weapon forged for a datu.

Taking a deep breath, I stepped beneath the shadow of the trees.

As I walked into the forest, it felt like something was leeching the warmth from the air. I thought I heard strange voices echoing through the trees.

It's just crickets, Tani. I shook my head before my imagination could terrify me further. *Serpent Riders aren't afraid of the dark.*

It wasn't long before I had the peculiar sensation that I'd been here before. Of course, I walked this exact same path in my vision in Babaylan Kalan-ya's house. Fireflies darted through the leaves—or were they glowing eyes, watching my every move?

The back of my neck prickled. Then my foot snagged on a tree root and I crashed to the ground.

"Ah. A visitor."

I froze, hand halfway to my sword as a shadow fell over me. A cloaked woman loomed above, silhouetted in the light of a flickering campfire. Beneath her hood, two bright eyes gleamed.

"What do we have here?" she crooned. "A little girl got lost in the woods?"

I clamped down the fear that flickered up my back and got to my feet. "I'm not lost. I came here to find you."

The woman pulled back her hood to release waves of ebony hair. Her smile was golden.

I got the sudden feeling she had known all along that I would come tonight.

Fighting down unease, I kept my voice as steady as I could. "I brought everything you asked for." The walis tingting, the jar of charcoal, and the blue cone shell dropped to the ground. "Now, hold up your end of the bargain."

Mutya laughed. "People have often spoken ill of me, but know this: I never turn back on a promise."

Beckoning, Mutya led me to the fire, which I was alarmed to see glowed purple instead of amber.

"Life is not created lightly," she warned. "That is the way of the world. Nothing is created without something first being destroyed."

There was a hypnotic quality about Mutya's gaze that made it difficult to look away. "What does that mean?"

"It means there is a price to pay. As there is with everything. Are you sure you want to proceed?"

I thought of Bato, who would jeer at me when I showed up tomorrow without a bakunawa. Of Kiri, who might not even want to be friends with me now that he could properly spar with the other novices. And then I thought of Ligaya.

Even now, I shuddered at the thought of what would have happened if Bato and Iska hadn't rescued her. If they hadn't swept in at the last moment, Ligaya would be one more cold figure lying beside the Serpent Riders we lost that night.

I had been standing *right there*—and for all my warrior training, I had been worse than helpless.

If I'd had a bakunawa, I could have kept my sister safe. I could have protected her.

I made my choice.

"My mother has lots of gold at our house. Whatever the price is, I will pay it."

Mutya chuckled. An expression flickered over her face—was it pity?

"All right," she said. "Let's begin."

Suddenly, shadows stretched from the trees, gathering around my feet. The wind became the murmur of thousands of voices that rushed past my ears.

Mutya took the walis tingting and smeared it with charcoal from the jar, staining the palm leaves black.

I pointed at the blue cone shell left on the ground. "What about the shell?"

Mutya gave me a knowing smile but didn't answer. Instead, her voice took on a rhythmic, chanting tone.

"Cast life into the lifeless; give breath to that which does not breathe."

Mutya threw the soot-smeared broom in the fire. I staggered back, coughing, as the flames flared bright and a puff of ash burst into the air.

When I dared open my eyes, I saw there was a new being in the clearing—a sleek, serpentine form with black scales, its burning eyes fixed on me.

A bakunawa.

As I stared at it in shock, I became aware of another change. My mind felt different somehow, split in two, as another consciousness was laid on top of mine.

"Go on," Mutya murmured. "He doesn't bite."

Cautiously, I stepped closer. The jet-black bakunawa regarded me unblinkingly, its fins rippling as it hovered in the air. I reached toward it. The bakunawa flinched back, a hiss building deep in its throat.

I was surprised when I felt its fear flash through my own mind—tense and restless.

"It's all right," I found myself saying. "I won't hurt you."

Some of my calmness must have reached through our bond, because the bakunawa visibly relaxed. It drifted over to me, bumping its head against my knuckles. Its scales were faintly warm.

"It looks real enough, but it does not have the same life essence as a true living creature. That means it has weaknesses." Mutya looked at me. "Your bakunawa is nothing but ash given breath. The spell will unravel if you—and only you—say the counterspell: 'breath to ash.'"

I almost laughed in relief. I could never imagine willingly commanding my bakunawa to unravel, so the chance of me saying the counterspell was nonexistent.

Pushing that knowledge to the back of my mind, I cast

an appraising glance over my new bakunawa. Usually, a serpent's color indicated which element they could wield, but I'd never seen a black bakunawa before.

I pointed to a stick on the ground. "Incinerate," I commanded, trying not to get my hopes up.

The bakunawa looked at the stick, then back at me, a question in its eyes.

Not fire, then. I hid my disappointment. "Throw the stick to me."

The bakunawa circled the stick. Slowly but surely, the stick slid across the ground like it was being dragged by an invisible force, coming to a stop by my feet.

"Air?" I blinked. There hadn't been any wind.

Mutya regarded the stick thoughtfully. "It looks like the bakunawa can bend shadows to its will."

"Shadows?" I repeated. According to Swordmaster Pai, a bakunawa could only wield one of four elemental magics: fire, water, earth, or air. I never thought shadow bakunawa even existed.

"It is a rare power," Mutya said, "but not unheard of. Your bakunawa can grab hold of any shadow—whether belonging to a person, animal, plant, or object—and control it. When the shadow is manipulated, the object that cast the shadow is forced to follow suit. Your serpent took hold of the stick's shadow and pulled *that* toward you, and since objects are inseparable from their shadows, the stick simply followed along."

I frowned, trying to understand.

Mutya tapped her chin. "Shadow manipulation gives your bakunawa a power far greater than any of the elemental magics, with the ability to move almost anything it wishes—as long as the object casts a shadow, of course. It can even *stop* things from moving by pinning their shadows in place. Think of it like a puppet master pulling the strings of his figurines, only the strings are the shadows, and the puppet master is . . . well, your bakunawa."

Curiosity sparked inside me. My serpent was different for sure, but it wouldn't be that hard to disguise my bakunawa's shadow power as being related to the air. Together, we'd be a fighting force to be reckoned with.

Now I could finally fight against the monsters that threatened my home. I could protect our moon when Great Bakunawa returned. I could keep Ligaya safe.

"I still have to give you a name," I told the bakunawa. Its eyes remained fixed on me, glowing like embers in a bed of coal. The name came to me immediately. "Uling."

As soon as I spoke the word, a rush of emotions flooded over me—like a part of me that I'd always known was missing had been found.

Never mind my own bakunawa egg, which stubbornly refused to hatch—Uling and I were bound by a force far beyond what could be described with words. At my call, he would answer. And I would come to his aid as willingly as he would come to mine.

The bakunawa—*my* bakunawa—growled happily, settling around my shoulders like a cloak. Through our bond,

I felt Uling's own excitement at our new companionship. More than that, I sensed a fire inside him—a burning need to fight, to *win*. It was a mirror to the fire that burned inside of me.

A fierce grin spread across my face. I felt brave. I felt invincible. I felt like a Serpent Rider.

"Thank you," I told Mutya, meaning it. "I don't know how I can repay you."

Mutya smiled, showing all her teeth. "Don't worry, I know the perfect way. Very soon, I will return to collect my due."

Chapter 6

My feet crunched across the sand as the waves whispered over the beach. The sun had barely even risen, but I wanted to get to training early.

Since the berberoka attack two nights before, I had noticed several villagers glancing warily toward the ocean, half expecting another berberoka to emerge from the calm water at any moment. Now I could prove to everyone that I really *was* a warrior. That I could protect our village and our moon, just like my father would have done.

Energy thrummed through my body. I spied the novices heading down to the beach. As always, Bato was in the lead, with Iska flying behind him like a copper banner. My rival looked surprised to see me so early, but then his mouth stretched into a nasty smile. "Someone's excited to lose today."

I met him with a smile of my own. "Who is?"

Uling slithered out from behind me, scales gleaming in the sun. His eyes smoldered like embers.

Bato stopped in his tracks. *"What?"*

As the rest of the novices arrived with their bakunawa, several shocked glances were sent Uling's way.

Kiri ran down the sand with Luntian beside him. As soon as Luntian saw Uling, the smaller bakunawa shrank behind Kiri's back.

"Tani," my friend breathed, his eyes wide in admiration. "He looks *magnificent*."

I was always grateful to have Kiri cheering me on, but even better was seeing that Bato was nowhere near as smug as usual now that I had a bakunawa. Perhaps he'd always known that I was a better fighter than him.

Scowling, Bato shouldered my friend aside. "When did it hatch?"

"Last night," I answered, going for a half-truth. When I returned from the forest last night, I made sure to hide my real bakunawa egg where no one would ever find it.

Iska circled Uling menacingly, her forked tongue flicking at the newcomer. I desperately hoped she wouldn't sense that Uling wasn't all he appeared to be.

Bato still wasn't convinced. "He's a little big for a new hatchling, isn't he?"

Uling *was* bigger than the average bakunawa. Already, he was almost the same size as Iska, who was two years old.

I shrugged. "He has to start out strong if he's going to fight for our moon, right?"

Bato glanced at his arm. To my horror, I saw that his skin was streaked with soot from where he'd accidentally brushed against Uling.

Bato wrinkled his nose. "He needs a wash too."

Before my rival could ask any more questions, Swordmaster Pai appeared out of the training lodge. As usual, he wore his glittering serpent-scale armor with his war golok strapped over his shoulder. He clapped his hands, silencing our chatter.

His sharp gaze focused on Uling and me, betraying surprise. Biting my lip, I willed myself to keep a straight face in front of my teacher.

After a long, tense silence, he spoke. "We will not be sparring today. The tragic attack two nights ago proved that we must be prepared to protect our village from every threat at every moment. As you know, what makes the Serpent Riders great warriors is their unbreakable connection with their bakunawa. Now that we all have serpent companions"—he cast another bewildered glance at me—"these bonds will be put to the test."

Instead of sending us to the sparring area, our teacher directed us to the far end of the beach, where I helped the other novices construct a row of small pyramids out of old coconut husks. About thirty feet in front of the pyramids, Swordmaster Pai used the end of his sword to score a line in the sand.

"From behind the line, your bakunawa will use their elemental powers to knock over a pyramid.

Whoever collapses their pyramid first will be declared the victor."

Bato smirked at me as we took our places. He knew that he had the advantage of years of training with his bakunawa, while I'd only had mine for less than a day.

I wasn't sure of Uling's full capabilities, but I wanted more than anything to prove my rival wrong.

"Fire!" Swordmaster Pai shouted.

The air exploded with energy. Gusts of wind from air bakunawa whooshed past me, while water bakunawa shot torrents of water that missed the coconut husks by a mere handsbreadth. Fire blasted forward in hopes of simply incinerating the pyramids. I thought the earth bakunawa would dominate this challenge, but it was proving difficult to quake the sand beneath the target pyramid without toppling over everyone else's as well.

"Luntian! Go!" Red-faced, Kiri tried to direct Luntian's magic, but the short time they'd been together proved itself. The bakunawa's fins rippled in confusion before a sheer curtain of water formed in front of him. Luntian flicked his tail, but instead of the water being sent toward the pyramid, the suspended droplets exploded, showering onto Kiri's head.

I was unable to suppress a smile. I'd never been able to participate in a challenge involving elemental magic—and now, I would win my very first one.

"What's wrong?" Bato teased from further down the line

when he saw that Uling hadn't done anything yet. "Did your bakunawa leave his powers behind in his eggshell?"

The top three husks of Bato's pyramid had already been burned clean off by Iska's well-aimed currents of fire.

Ignore him, I thought, rolling my eyes. *Catch the shadow, Uling.*

My serpent had been looping restlessly in the air, just waiting for me to give him the chance. I didn't see his power so much as *feel* it—I was suddenly aware of the shadows of every person, bakunawa, and object on the beach. I imagined my stack of coconut husks falling over.

Uling tugged at the shadow beneath the pyramid.

The husks wobbled—and then the pyramid came crashing down.

The roar of elemental magic died away as everyone saw that the challenge was finished. The other novices stared at me, wide-eyed. Bato's jaw was practically touching the sand.

"Challenge over," called Swordmaster Pai. As he glanced at the scattered coconut husks, even he looked surprised at how quickly his task had been beaten. "With the objective successfully completed, the victor is . . . Tanikala!"

There were a few more moments of shocked silence before Kiri began to chant my name. Soon, almost everyone else was clapping along.

A slow grin spread across my face. With my fighting skills and Uling's shadow magic, we were unstoppable.

The only person who wasn't cheering was Bato, whose face was stony. Over his shoulder, Iska growled, her eyes fixed on Uling.

I waved at Bato with a smug smile. *You can't always be the hero.*

I turned as someone approached.

"Congratulations," said Swordmaster Pai. "I should have expected that the daughter of Datu Dakila would have a formidable air bakunawa by her side. Your father and I trained together as novices, and I don't think even he could have beaten that challenge so soon after Buhawi hatched."

I let out a tiny breath of relief—he thought Uling had knocked over the pyramid with a gust of air.

"I was surprised too," I replied, feeling guilty about lying to a man who upheld honor more than anything. "Uling and I will make a good team."

My teacher nodded thoughtfully. "I see your father in you, Tanikala. Our moon is in good hands."

That was the highest praise, but knowing what I'd done only made me feel guiltier.

After we'd cleaned up the mess, Swordmaster Pai called us back to the training lodge. It looked like he was going to make an announcement. I glanced at Kiri curiously, who was still drenched in water, wondering what it could be.

"With wicked, heartless monsters teeming in the forests and the seas, it is now more important than ever that we raise the next generation of Serpent Riders."

We all stood up a little straighter at his words. All of us

wanted to be Serpent Riders more than anything, slaying the foul creatures that dared attack our home.

But it was one thing to dream of becoming fierce fighters, and something completely different to consider what it really meant, especially with the berberoka attack still fresh in our minds.

"That is why I have decided to hold the Warrior Trial, so that you all have the chance to prove yourselves worthy of your serpents and your swords."

There was a moment of shock, and then excited murmurs rippled around me. Holding a Warrior Trial this early—when all of us only had a few years of training, not when we were grown up—was unheard of. But after the berberoka wiped out three veteran warriors, we desperately needed more Serpent Riders in case another monster attacked. I couldn't blame Swordmaster Pai for his decision.

I looked at Kiri and saw my own eagerness, along with a healthy dose of anxiety, reflected in his eyes. The swordmaster's Warrior Trial would separate the true warriors from the novices, as those who passed the trial became full-fledged Serpent Riders. The challenge was different every time it was held, but one thing was sure—all our grueling months of training would finally be put to the test.

Our teacher waited for us to fall quiet before he continued.

"The trial will begin exactly seven days from now, at sunrise. Don't be late."

☾

That night, the village was abuzz. In front of our house, a fire glowed, over which a whole pig roasted on a spit. Its skin was golden brown and crispy, cooked to perfection. People passed around bamboo plates heaped with rice mixed with toasted garlic.

Just like Kiri's celebration, Datu Eeya was holding a party to commemorate Uling's hatch day. When my mother found out I had a bakunawa, she'd looked at me strangely—as if she couldn't believe my egg had hatched so suddenly. I thought I did a good job of deflecting any questions about the missing eggshells by telling my mother I'd already thrown them into the sea as was our custom, but I noticed her glancing at Uling every now and again.

Eventually, though, it became clear that the villagers expected a celebration. As the datu, my mother had put everything into tonight that the village could afford. I felt incredibly grateful—and more than a little special.

Do you really deserve this, Tani? whispered a small voice in my head. *Everyone is cheering for a bakunawa that doesn't really exist . . .*

Grimacing, I pushed the voice down into the darkest corner of my mind until I couldn't hear it at all.

The memory of the berberoka attack still hung over the beach like a clinging shadow, but Uling's birthday was the perfect opportunity for the villagers to have the party they hadn't been able to finish two nights before. Even Bato was here, and I'd never seen anything so entertaining as Bato forcing himself to look happy for me with everyone watching.

The only one missing was Ligaya, who had been ecstatic when I'd introduced her to Uling. Knowing she would be watching, I waved in the direction of her window.

Veteran Serpent Riders came up to congratulate me. Even their bakunawa seemed happy as they wolfed down their favorite food—fish freshly caught from the sea.

A few older villagers were sitting around the fire, barely able to contain their excitement as they beamed at me with gap-toothed smiles. They were old enough to remember the last time Great Bakunawa returned, and they held horrible memories of how the Moon Eater rose from the sea, causing the earth to quake in terror as she devoured the moon. Ever since my father died, their faces had been shadowed by despair—but now that my bakunawa was here, the hope rekindled in their eyes. With Uling by my side, *nothing* would destroy our last moon. I'd make sure of it.

"Tanikala."

I turned at my mother's voice. She stood with a plate of food in her hands, but it looked untouched.

"Swordmaster Pai told me about the challenge this morning, and how you were the victor."

I nodded, throat tight. Would my mother see through my ruse?

Datu Eeya glanced at Uling. The coal-black serpent almost blended into the night. Perhaps she saw a shadow of Buhawi in him.

I felt the weight of her expectation press down on me. Under great pressure as the village leader, my mother had always been cold and distant, but I knew she wanted me to be a brave warrior like my father.

Since the day I was born, I had let her down more times than I could count.

Now, she could finally be proud of me.

"I heard he is an air bakunawa, like your father's." For some reason, my mother's voice was strained.

I grinned. "Isn't he beautiful?"

Datu Eeya nodded. The corners of her mouth twitched as if she was trying to smile but something was holding her back. I expected her to congratulate me, but instead, she kept gazing at Uling with the oddest expression—a mixture of wonder and disbelief.

I felt my blood rise. After Bato had mocked me for years, saying that I couldn't possibly save the moon without a bakunawa, after Ligaya had almost *died* when the ber-beroka attacked—my mother's indifference toward me and Uling was just too much.

The words exploded out of me before I could stop them. "I've done everything you asked for! I trained as a warrior with Swordmaster Pai, and now I have my own bakunawa. Can't you even be a little bit proud of me?"

I instantly regretted my outburst as my mother's lips

drew into a thin, pale line. A tense silence followed, and I noticed a few Serpent Riders nervously glance toward us. No one would dare speak to the datu in such a way.

My mother steepled her hands. Without a word, she turned and vanished into the smoke.

Chapter 7

The day of the Warrior Trial dawned gray and brooding, the first hint of a storm on the horizon. The sky perfectly matched the novices' moods as we waited on the beach— ready to fight with a force like thunder, but still troubled about what the day would bring. After all, we'd seen with our own eyes what it was truly like to fight a monster—and the devastation that followed no matter how skilled the warriors were.

Kiri was the first to arrive. Over the past week, I'd seen him working on his own fighting moves and on Luntian's control of elemental magic. Considering he'd only had his bakunawa for a short time compared to the others, I was impressed with his progress.

They would make a formidable pair—but they weren't as good as me and Uling.

Bato stood among his circle of friends, joking and laughing. Despite his carefree attitude, I caught him sneaking furtive glances toward me. That was good. It meant he saw me as a threat to his victory, not the weak pushover he liked to claim I was.

At sunrise, Swordmaster Pai arrived. He placed a wooden statue, carved into the likeness of a crouching person, on the sand.

"Today's Warrior Trial will take place in the forest. As usual, the trial will be held within the area deemed safe by our scouts, marked out by red flags." Our teacher indicated the statue at his feet. "The objective is simple. Three statues identical to this one are hidden throughout the trial zone. The first three novices to retrieve a statue and return to me will be crowned as victors and brand-new Serpent Riders."

We glanced at each other in nervous anticipation. Swordmaster Pai made the challenge sound like our typical training, but today, there was so much more riding on a victory than bragging rights.

All I had to do was win this trial, and I would be a Serpent Rider.

Swordmaster Pai gestured, and we all turned to face the trees.

"Ready, set, *go!*"

We bolted in a flurry of kicked-up sand. As soon as we reached the forest, we scattered. Some novices searched close to the ground, while others shimmied up tree trunks to try and get a bird's-eye view.

I realized how difficult our teacher's challenge really was.

It was just like our wily swordmaster to hide statues made of wood in a *forest*.

This is impossible. How is searching for a statue supposed to make us better warriors?

Clods of dirt exploded around me as earth bakunawa dug beneath the ground in search of the prize. I ran past them with Uling flying behind me. His shadow power wouldn't be much help in the search, but I hadn't spent years of training doing nothing.

I gazed at the leaf-shrouded treetops. Swordmaster Pai wouldn't have hidden the statues where we could easily grab them—they had to be in places that could only be reached by strength and skill. And yet, he didn't expect us to waste our time turning over every leaf and pebble. To be a real test of our warrior skills, the statues needed to be someplace where we'd have to fight the elements, and each other, to secure the win.

Reaching up, I grasped a knob in a trunk and started climbing. I searched through the leaves for any sign of a statue, but found nothing.

I made it to the top of the tree and peered across the forest. One tree towered far above the rest—a mighty balete that was said to be two hundred years old, its crown a maze of tangled branches.

A statue *had* to be up there.

An idea popped into my head. Concentrating hard, I leaped from my tree in a flurry of leaves and landed squarely on the branches of the next. I hoped that hopping from tree to tree would keep me hidden from the rest of the novices, letting me reach the balete without being attacked.

Suddenly, the wind quickened, tugging at my limbs and threatening to topple me from my perch.

Clinging on tight, I saw another novice crouching in a nearby tree, his air bakunawa flicking its tail and working its magic. If I jumped now, the strong wind would fling me to the ground. After all, the rules never said we couldn't sabotage other novices during the hunt—it was all part of our training.

Well, I thought grimly, *I can fight back too.*

I glanced at Uling, coiled around a branch to keep from being blown away, and sent him a thought-command. Uling bared his fangs.

The air bakunawa froze as Uling immobilized its shadow, and as quickly as it had started, the driving wind died down. The enemy novice reached for his sword, surprised—then outraged when he found out that he was frozen too.

Even though Mutya had already explained Uling's power, I couldn't believe that he had thwarted my opponent so easily. Mutya was right—shadow magic gave me an undeniable advantage over the other novices.

I smiled. *Well done, Uling.* Victory was as good as ours.

When I reached the balete, six other novices who had the same idea were already scurrying up the trunk like spindly spiders.

I scrambled over walls of knotted roots to join them and latched onto the rough bark, quickly outpacing everyone else as I climbed hand over hand.

Gusts of wind tugged at my clothes as I was attacked with bakunawa magic. Showers of dirt poured on top of me, and some challengers even sent bursts of fire to try and intimidate me into backing down. But I directed Uling to freeze my attackers long enough for me to climb out of their range. It didn't matter how long the others had trained alongside their bakunawa—they were all helpless in the face of Uling's magic, as surely as each was bound to their shadow.

Together, Uling and I were undefeatable.

I made it to the thick tangle of leaves at the top of the tree, shadows enveloping me in a cool blanket. To my surprise, the leaves shivered with the presence of another novice.

I was even more surprised to see that it was Kiri.

Of course, I thought with a smile. While other warriors used their brawn to win challenges, Kiri was more inclined to use his brain. He'd probably known to go straight to the balete tree as soon as the trial started.

With Uling's darker coloring, it was easier to stay hidden as I looked in every gnarled knot and hollow for the statue.

Kiri suddenly squealed in delight. "Luntian, it's here."

I glanced up and saw what Kiri had seen first. A wooden statue was cradled in the fork of two branches, just waiting for someone to take it.

Kiri climbed the branches cautiously, but with his small frame, he had trouble reaching the higher handholds without knocking the statue off the branch and making it tumble to the ground below.

I grinned. The statue was mine.

I was about to pull its shadow toward me with a silent command to Uling—then I paused.

No, Uling, I thought. *Give it to Kiri.*

Uling obediently pulled the statue's shadow in the opposite direction. The statue teetered precariously before falling right into Kiri's waiting hands.

My friend stared at it in disbelief. Then with a wide grin, he tucked it into his sash, out of sight. With a flick of branches, he disappeared.

I quickly climbed back down. I still had time to find another statue, and the look on Bato's face when he saw not one, but two underdogs coming home with the win would be worth losing this one.

I leaped to the ground and started running. There was one more place I thought a statue could be hidden.

There was a clearing where the trees opened out to a broad lake. The water was turquoise, crystal clear. If the sun had been out today, the rays of light would have glittered on its surface like daytime stars.

Swordmaster Pai always made us do water exercises here, like seeing who could hold their breath longest, swim farthest, or dive deepest. A Serpent Rider had to know how to fight in water as well as on land.

I glanced around, half hoping to see a statue embedded in the white sand along the shore.

You need to go higher. I clambered up a tall rock formation, using the height advantage to survey the entire lake.

There—wedged between two rocks at the bottom of the lake, half buried in sand, was a statue.

My spirit sang. The only problem was that it was underwater, meaning I needed to dive to retrieve it. And I could already hear other novices moving through the trees. I had to be fast.

"Stay here," I commanded Uling. "You can guard this." I untied my sash, letting my father's sword drop onto the rocks. The weapon would only weigh me down.

My toes curled over the rock's edge and I took a deep breath.

Then I dived.

Cool water closed around my body as I glided through the lake. I opened my eyes, blinking to let my vision adjust. Schools of tiny fish darted away, startled.

Breathing out slowly, I kicked downward and swam toward the statue. *Not too fast, or you'll run out of air.* I gave up on trying to yank the statue out and started digging around it. Plumes of sand drifted into the water, clouding my vision.

Finally, something gave way beneath my hands. *Yes.* With a last heave, the statue came away and into my grasp. Resisting the urge to laugh, I instead clutched it tight to my chest.

Now to return to Swordmaster Pai. I pushed off from the sandy floor, kicking my way back to the surface.

Suddenly, a shadow moved across the water, speeding toward me as fast as an arrow.

I frantically tried to kick away. But then the figure was on me, arms wrapping around me, trying to wrestle the statue from my grasp.

Amidst the surge of bubbles, I saw his face.

Bato.

Clamping down the urge to suck in air, I let the statue go. I didn't have breath to waste on an underwater fight. As soon as my rival had the prize in his grip, he surged back toward the surface.

I clenched my teeth, swimming after him as fast as I could. *That statue is mine.*

My head burst out of the water and I drew in deep breaths of air. Bato had almost reached the shore.

"Uling," I yelled, waving at my bakunawa still by the rocks. *Slow him down. And bring me my sword.*

The dark serpent raced toward the lake, my sword in its rattan scabbard clenched in his jaws. Bato flinched away as Uling's sharp tail slapped the water right in front of him. Swimming as fast as my tired muscles would allow, I closed the distance between us.

Thunder rolled in the distant sky. *I have to be faster.*

Bato dived beneath Uling's lashing tail, but I'd already caught up to him. I tackled him as he made it to the shore. We went down in a tangle of limbs and water spray.

We fought for a while, but neither of us managed to get the upper hand—Bato was trying to squirm out of my grip, and I wasn't letting him leave with the statue.

Bato narrowed his eyes. "Iska!"

A blaze of fire roared past my head, its heat blasting my skin dry. My grip loosened for only a moment, but that was enough for Bato to slam a hand into my gut, driving the wind from my body.

Uling leaped forward, but I stopped him with a sharp mental command.

I could call on his help if I needed it, but now, I wanted to prove that I really *was* a better fighter than Bato.

As my opponent got up to run away, I grabbed my kampilan and slammed the scabbard into his shins. Bato went down with an outraged yell. Before he could rise, I rolled to my feet and placed the tip of my sword against his heart.

"Yield," I said.

He blinked in disbelief before his face settled into its familiar scowl.

"Yield," I repeated. "Or are you going to call on Iska to finish the fight for you?"

Bato's mouth worked as he was about to say something nasty, but I knew he couldn't stand losing his honor. Scowling, he dropped the statue at my feet.

I stepped away and let him go. I didn't take my eyes off him until he and Iska disappeared back into the forest.

"We did it," I breathed, realizing I hadn't believed it until

I said it out loud. I turned the statue over in my hands as a wide grin stretched across my face.

Slinging my sword over my shoulder, I called, "Let's go, Uling."

It was time to become a Serpent Rider.

Chapter 8

When I got back to the training ground, Kiri was already standing beside Swordmaster Pai. My friend still looked stunned that he'd managed to return with a statue.

Kiri's face broke into a smile as he saw me approach with my prize held high.

"Look at us, Tani!" he said excitedly. "The last two to hatch their bakunawa are the first to win the trial!"

Soon, someone else joined us. I wasn't surprised that it was Bato. He carried a statue—probably stolen after a fight with whoever found it first—but his face was as thunderous as the sky overhead.

Swordmaster Pai beamed as Bato sullenly took his place beside us. Our teacher put two fingers to his lips and blew a series of loud whistles that sounded like bird calls, telling the novices still in the forest that the trial was over.

"Three victors," our teacher said proudly. "Three new Serpent Riders."

My entire being sang at the praise. This was what I was destined for.

Swordmaster Pai was about to say more, but then his eyes darted to a point over our shoulders. I turned to see someone running toward the beach.

It's my mother, I thought at the same time Kiri gasped.

Datu Eeya sprinted toward us like all the monsters of the Lower World were chasing her. It shocked us all to see the leader of our village, who was usually the picture of poise and grace, in such a state.

Even more shocking was the panic in her voice as she shouted, "Princess Ligaya is gone!"

As she spoke, a flash of lightning lit up the sky. The storm finally rolled in and sparse droplets fell, making tiny craters in the sand. The words washed over me like dark waves.

The triumph I'd felt after winning the trial suddenly vanished. *This can't be happening.*

Swordmaster Pai caught my mother's shoulders as she began sobbing uncontrollably.

"Have you searched the village?" Swordmaster Pai asked worriedly.

The datu nodded. "I've already sent out warriors to look for her, and I have people stationed at every entrance."

Our bakunawa shifted restlessly as the wind quickened. By now, all the novices had returned, and we stood around the datu and swordmaster in an uneasy circle.

"They haven't found her," Datu Eeya whispered. "My daughter is gone."

The words sounded unreal. I didn't understand how Ligaya could have just *disappeared*. My sister could be impulsive, but she wasn't reckless. If she knew the datu had sent a search party after her, she would've taken the hint and gone back home.

Unless . . .

An image of Mutya's pale face wreathed in smoke swam through my head. Before I knew it, I was tearing across the sand with Uling on my heels.

By the time I got home, my breath was sawing through my throat. I took the steps of the front ladder three at a time and burst into Ligaya's room.

My sister should have been sitting there, reciting a story or weaving at her loom. But the room was empty, and the sight hit me like a berberoka's punch.

Breathing hard, I wildly cast around for any trace of Ligaya. Her window was locked from the inside. She couldn't have snuck out that way.

Then I spotted a flash of color underneath Ligaya's loom. It was the rainbow feather I'd seen her weaving with.

The sight of it was more than unsettling. Ligaya *never* left anything out of place.

Shaking now, I slowly walked back outside. My mother, Swordmaster Pai, and several Serpent Riders had formed a ring around our house. Nervous villagers peeked out from nearby windows.

I knew we were all thinking the same thing. Although

my blood curdled at the thought, there was only one possible explanation.

She's been taken.

"How?" I shouted into the silence. Beside me, Uling flicked his tail in restless circles. "How did no one see her leave?"

At that moment, lightning blazed across the sky, turning the world into shades of black and white.

Datu Eeya gasped. "Ligaya!"

We all whirled, staring in the direction of my mother's pointing finger.

I couldn't believe what I was seeing. Ligaya stood framed between the wooden stilts of two houses, as if she'd just been out for a stroll.

Most of the villagers were momentarily taken aback at the sight of her, since this was the first time they'd seen the veiled princess. But as her sister, I instinctively knew something was horribly wrong.

Her eyes screamed, *Help me, Tani!* Though she stared straight ahead, unmoving, I sensed the terror in her gaze.

Before I could take a single step, someone else reached Ligaya first. The woman who appeared from the shadows had hair as black as night with a face as pale as the moon. She placed a hand on Ligaya's shoulder—claiming my sister as her own.

All the breath rushed out of my chest.

"Mutya," I whispered.

Although everyone was staring at her in horror, Mutya only looked at me. Her mouth tilted into a crooked smile.

Swordmaster Pai shouted, "Serpent Riders, attack!"

Blades hissed out of their sheaths and bakunawa bared their fangs as the warriors prepared to charge Mutya.

But the attack never came. Instead, every single warrior was rooted to the spot. Even Swordmaster Pai stood frozen with his blade half drawn, like he was more statue than man.

Mutya's dark gaze never left mine. Between flashes of lightning, I saw her hands twitch like she was plucking the strings of an instrument.

Realization hit me. *She's binding their shadows!*

No wonder Ligaya looked so strange—Mutya was holding her shadow too, making her unable to move, to run. All the Serpent Riders and their bakunawa were rendered completely powerless by Mutya's spell.

Wait . . .

I tried to step forward. To my surprise, my muscles obeyed me.

I can still move!

I didn't know what part of Mutya's spell had gone wrong for me to still be free while everyone else was trapped, but I wouldn't waste a moment longer. Drawing my sword, I charged at Mutya with a battle cry.

I hadn't even come within striking range when a dark shape slammed into me. The impact knocked me to the ground, pain sparking up my back.

My eyes focused on the shape looming above. "Uling?"

The bakunawa met my gaze, no hint of friendliness in his eyes, which now burned red as lava. Uling stretched his jaws, revealing razor teeth.

Behind Uling, Mutya's smile widened as she bent her finger like a puppet master pulling a string.

Deep within me, I felt my bond with my bakunawa—if it had ever existed to begin with—unravel like the torn threads of a once-shining tapestry. Uling was now entirely under Mutya's control, just as he had always been.

Too stunned to react, I couldn't even brace myself as the shadow bakunawa streaked toward me at Mutya's command, teeth glinting.

Air rushed into my face as Uling shot past. I spun around to see that Uling wasn't aiming for me—instead, he was angling right toward Swordmaster Pai's exposed neck.

"Uling, stop!" I yelled, even though I knew my words would do nothing.

Swordmaster Pai was frozen, utterly unable to defend himself from the certain death speeding toward him.

In those split seconds, my choice became blindingly clear. There was only one way to end this.

"Breath to ash!" I shouted.

Just before Uling's jaws could snap around the swordmaster's throat, the bakunawa convulsed as the counterspell took hold.

Uling's jet-black scales turned back into ordinary

palm-leaf fronds. The burning glow of his eyes faded into old charcoal that dropped, lifeless, onto the ground.

At that moment, the heavens opened. Rain crashed down, drenching us all.

Dropping to my knees in the mud, I grabbed the ruined objects that had once been Uling, that had once symbolized all my hopes and dreams. "No," I whispered, black rivulets of charcoal running between my fingers. *"No."*

Even though everyone was immobilized, I felt their gazes like sharp spears drilling into my back.

Mutya spared me from her shadow spell not because of any mistake, but because she wanted me to experience this humiliation and loss.

"Please," I said. "Please let us go."

Mutya waved a hand. "Oh, I've no need for you or these useless warriors. But this one"—she grinned at Ligaya—"I think I'll keep."

A chill deeper than the rain shivered through me.

"Why?" I whispered. "Uling is already gone. Why do you need to take Ligaya too?"

"I thought we came to an agreement," Mutya said simply. "You knew that you would lose your bakunawa as soon as you said those words. You also knew that I would be coming to collect my payment for our little spell—and the honored princess is the payment I choose." She shook her head like I was a naughty child needing to be taught a lesson. "I kept all my promises after all. Now it is time for you to keep yours."

The words died in my throat. In a terrible way, Mutya was right—she hadn't broken her word on *anything*. And I'd been played for a fool.

Even through the sheeting rain, Mutya's eyes burned like coal. One moment she was standing there, a hand on Ligaya's shoulder like my sister was some kind of trophy. Then I blinked, and they both disappeared—vanished between one flash of lightning and the next. Only the faint smell of sulfur wafted in their wake.

Once Mutya was gone, everyone suddenly stumbled forward as the grip on their shadows released. Swordmaster Pai's hands flew to his neck, as if he was unable to believe he was still alive.

Datu Eeya staggered to the spot where Ligaya had stood. Her face was deathly pale. The proud leader of our village now crouched in the mud and rain, distraught at her daughter's disappearance.

She finally saw the walis tingting in my hands, recognizing it as the exact same one that had sat in our house for years. Mutya's words hung in the air, proving my guilt to the whole village.

"Tanikala," my mother breathed. "What have you done?"

Those five words pierced into me deeper than any bakunawa's fang ever could.

Datu Eeya sank her face into her hands, past caring that her richly woven dress was thoroughly soaked. "Ligaya is gone. Taken by magic," she whispered. "Lost forever."

I could only kneel there as the rain crashed down on top of me along with the weight of an entire village's wrath.

"The princess is lost," came a croaking voice, "but not forever."

Babaylan Kalan-ya struggled through the rain, leaning on her wooden staff, her long hair blown back with the force of the wind. Everyone fell silent at her approach. The old woman radiated an invisible willpower—something not quite of this world.

Her face was stained black with soot from her seeing-smoke. Perhaps she'd been sitting by her fire ever since Ligaya went missing, leaning far into the fumes to delve into the future as deeply as she could.

"How is this even possible?" my mother demanded. "The talisman protects our village from dark magic, like it protected us from the berberoka!"

"It *did*," the old healer replied, looking straight at me. "But somebody stole it."

Realization crashed into me like a breaking wave. *The blue cone shell.* I couldn't believe the unremarkable-looking shell was actually the source of the powerful barrier that protected our village from evil creatures and enchantments.

I was sick with guilt at the memory of handing the shell to Mutya without a second thought. Free to use her powers, she could easily sneak into the village and make my sister disappear into thin air.

"Please, Babaylan," my mother pleaded. "Tell me how to bring Ligaya home."

The old woman's words were as fraught with warning as the booming thunder. *"If the princess you will find, break the chains that bind."*

I hadn't the faintest idea what that riddle meant. All I knew was that I let everyone down, especially my dear little sister—all because I tried to cheat my way to being a Serpent Rider. Mutya should have taken me instead.

Fighting back tears, I staggered to my feet and ran.

I didn't know where I was going—probably to find Mutya, to bleed the life out of that lying hag.

Before I got very far, two Serpent Riders grabbed my arms. I struggled against them—kicking, biting, screaming out my rage—but I was no match for their strength. They hefted me like a sack of rice and carried me back home.

Datu Eeya was waiting by the door. "Take her up," she commanded, her voice as cold as a mountain stream. "I want two people around this house at all times. She is not to leave until the princess is found."

The Serpent Riders dumped me roughly on the floor before heading back outside to stand guard. I ran to the window and stared at my mother, doing everything I could not to shout.

My mother met my eyes, her face impassive. As she turned away, I saw her glance toward where I knew the carved statue of my father stood. Her eyes betrayed a flicker of sadness.

I stomped across my room and kicked the wall so hard the wood shuddered. I breathed in and out as Swordmaster Pai had taught me, struggling to master my emotions.

By the time I returned to the window, my mother was gone.

Chapter 9

That night, I paced restlessly around my room as light rain pattered on the roof.

Creak. Creak. Creak. The wooden floorboards protested beneath each step. If my mother was here, she'd have scolded me for being so loud. But she was likely still waiting in the rain, anxious for Ligaya's return.

A pang of guilt pierced me for what seemed like the thousandth time. I finally admitted to myself that meeting Mutya had been an act of pure selfishness and I hadn't thought about the consequences.

Some Serpent Rider you would've been, Tani.

The more I thought about my little sister—who'd never learned how to fend for herself in the wild—somewhere out there, lost and afraid, the more agonized I became.

I'd felt like this only once before—two years ago, when Ligaya tried to sneak out of the house on her own for the first time. She had discovered she could climb out the back window and leap into the forest beyond. I'd come home early from training that day and was mortified to find my sister gone. Feeling the same cold sense of dread squeezing my chest, I rushed off to find her without even thinking to tell our mother.

After hours of searching, I eventually found her at the cliffs by the beach, where she'd fallen down a gap between two slabs of rock while exploring the salt-bleached crags. She'd been stuck there most of the morning, too far from the village to call for help—and to make matters worse, the tide was rising fast.

I threw my sash down for Ligaya to grab, but she wasn't strong enough to pull herself up, and the rock was too slippery for her to climb. Knowing that we were running out of time, I did the only thing I could think of.

I jumped down into the rising water and balanced Ligaya on my shoulders until she clambered to safety. Then I climbed out all alone, scraping my shins on the rock and splashing back into the water more times than I could count. When I finally managed to escape, beaten and bruised and stinging with salt, I wanted to yell at my sister for almost getting us both killed.

But I was surprised to find myself squeezing Ligaya in a tight hug because I was just happy beyond words that she was safe. Ligaya was more than just my sister. She was my first—and back then, only—friend.

On that day, I promised to always protect her no matter

what. But now Ligaya was lost again. And this time, it was entirely my fault.

I shook my head and paced faster, forcing myself to think of practical things. That was one of Swordmaster Pai's rules: *Worry about today, not yesterday.* My one consolation was that Babaylan Kalan-ya's cryptic words on the beach meant that my little sister was still alive, that someone could still find her.

As soon as my mother left, I'd dug my bakunawa egg out. While I was most angry with myself, the creature came a close second.

None of this would have happened if only you'd just hurried up.

But the irritation faded as quickly as it had come. It wasn't the bakunawa's fault it was taking so long to hatch.

If the Serpent Riders were looking for Ligaya, perhaps Kiri and Bato would be among them too. I was seething. Ligaya was *my* sister. *I* should have been in the forest searching for her.

But it's your fault she got lost in the first place.

Still, I had to do *something.* If I stayed trapped in here a moment longer, I would explode.

The two guards and their bakunawa were still outside. If I wanted to find my sister, I'd first have to get past them.

A breath of wind stirred the metal chimes hanging off the house next door, sending a faint tinkling into the air.

I stopped pacing as I came up with a plan.

Scooping up my egg, I tied it into my sash along with my water container, whetstone, and the half-empty jar of charcoal I'd brought to Mutya, which I could use for lighting campfires. Most importantly, I made sure my father's kampilan was fastened securely on my shoulders. Then I went into Ligaya's room.

Because she was the village princess, her room was far more richly furnished than mine. The walls were draped with fabrics she had woven, and on the floor were chests filled with fine clothes and boxes of gold jewelry. Pushing down a new wave of guilt, I sorted through my sister's possessions. Ligaya collected all kinds of things from her adventures to remind her of the outside world, and I knew there would be something here that would work perfectly for my plan.

A pearly shimmer caught my eye. Hidden behind Ligaya's loom was a collection of seashells and glimmering rocks.

I picked up a round pebble. It looked like any old rock, but peering closer, I saw glittering specks where tiny crystals were trapped inside it. That sounded like my little sister—able to see beauty in even the most ordinary things. *Even in me.*

I scooped up a handful of similar pebbles and went to the front window.

Sorry, Ligaya, I thought, peering across the way to the house opposite—and to the wind chimes that hung from its eaves. *Please forgive me. I'm trying to save you.*

Pulling back my arm, I took aim and flung a stone through the window.

The first throw missed, instead clattering noisily against the house's wooden wall. I heard an exclamation from below as my guards took notice. I waited for their attention to wander before pegging another pebble at our neighbor's house.

This time, the pebble slammed through one, two, three wind chimes, sending them ringing in a frantic flurry. When the guards went to investigate, I leaped onto the window ledge and swung myself smoothly onto the thatched roof.

The light drizzle chilled my shoulders as I ran.

I didn't hesitate as I reached the edge. Leaping, I jumped easily over the blockade wall and dropped silently into the dark forest.

Just like when I'd visited Mutya, the forest's shadows enveloped me in a sinister embrace. But the simmering anger in my chest boiled away the fear.

Mutya. I have to find Mutya. Though the clouds obscured the moon, some part of me instinctively knew where to go. I stomped through the shadows to where I knew the wandering woman's campsite was. When the foliage became too thick, I pulled out my sword and hacked at the leaves.

The final clinging branch fell away beneath my blade. I charged into the clearing, breathing hard, ready to grab Mutya and threaten her on the edge of my sword.

Instead, rain fell softly onto leaf-strewn dirt, quiet and peaceful.

There was nothing there.

"No," I whispered.

Even with the rain, I expected that *some* remnant of the campsite would be left behind. But it looked like Mutya had packed everything up and left. Or—even worse—like she was never even here to begin with.

But she has *been here. Ligaya is gone.*

I sank to my knees, leaning on my sword, as rain tracked down my face like the tears I was so unwilling to shed. The truth settled on me, colder than the night.

I failed as a warrior.

I failed as a Serpent Rider.

Most of all, I failed as an older sister.

I didn't know how long I stayed there, letting the rain do its best to wash away my misery. After a while, I looked up, not wanting to head home just yet.

And then a light glimmered through the trees.

I blinked, thinking it was my imagination. But then another one appeared beside it. Then another, and another, until the forest was aglow with fiery orbs. Like the stars had fallen to the earth.

Strangely, I didn't feel scared. One of the orbs started flickering. I squinted, not quite sure whether my eyes were playing tricks on me.

Ligaya.

The word was softer than a whisper, more in my mind than anywhere else. Stunned, I stepped closer.

The orb spun toward me. *Ligaya.*

"How do you know her name?" I breathed.

In reply, the spirit moved away, then closer, then away again. Its meaning was clear: *follow me.*

I hesitated, hand on my sword. I was still a novice, without a bakunawa to defend myself from the terrors of the forest. But whatever this spirit was, it must have known my sister. Perhaps it could lead me to Ligaya.

In the end, desperation won out.

I followed the dancing orb through the trees. Its kin watched silently as I slipped and scrambled over rocks and roots, my feet squelching in puddles. It dashed through the trees like a meteor, and I skidded after it as fast as I dared, squinting through the drizzle to keep the fire orb in sight. The forest grew thicker, and sharp branches swiped at my skin, and soon it was so dark that my hands were only pale shapes in front of me. But I kept going.

Suddenly, the orb stopped. Still running after it, I only discovered my mistake when the ground disappeared beneath my feet.

My stomach lurched as I fell into nothingness.

I flung out a hand, but my grasping fingers only slid over mud and stone. Far below, I heard the roar of rushing water.

Too late, I saw the flame spirit for what it really was. A lure.

It led me here to drown.

There was no time to regret my mistake. Drawing my sword, I drove it into the earth with all my strength.

The blade scraped against the cliff face as the sound of

roaring water grew louder. I held on as tight as I could, gritting my teeth as my numb hands threatened to slide off the hilt.

And then the blade bit and held. I hung on for dear life, shivering, as I dangled over nothing but air.

Chapter 10

My sword shifted beneath my weight, sending pebbles tumbling into the river. Resisting the urge to wipe my hair from my eyes, I desperately tried to find a way out.

If only I had a bakunawa, I thought bitterly. *It could've carried me to the ground.*

But I *didn't*. All I had to depend on was myself.

My sword suddenly tilted as the blade began to lose its perilous hold on the rocks. Before long, it would slide free . . . and that would be the end.

The flame spirit that led me here still hovered above my head, seemingly curious about my predicament. Lights appeared around me as more of the mischievous spirits came to watch me die.

I gripped my sword tighter, feeling my anger rise. I couldn't—*wouldn't*—let myself be beaten so easily by some nameless spirits that didn't even care about me. It couldn't end now. Not like this.

In the new light, I saw tall trees stretching up toward the cliff, their branches reaching out like spindly hands to catch me.

My sword jolted again. Any moment now, it would give way.

Moving as quickly as I dared, I reached for the first slender branch, my fingers closing over wet bark and sharp leaves.

Then my sword slipped free.

I gasped in terror as my senses swooped. I let go of my sword, which tumbled down into the shadows as I gripped the branch with both hands. Beneath my weight, the branch bent alarmingly, the sound of cracking splinters sawing through the air.

The branch snapped. I crashed into the branch right below it. Too winded to stop myself, I flopped between twigs and leaves before hitting the ground with a *whump*.

For a moment, I lay there staring at the sky. The fire spirits hovered for a moment longer, but after seeing that I'd made it out alive, they vanished in a puff of smoke.

Now I really was alone.

I got to my feet and limped over to retrieve my sword, where it was stuck in the soft ground point-first. *At least it didn't fall into the river,* I thought, glancing at the roaring stream gorged by the rain.

But now I had a different problem. I didn't have to look around to know that I had never seen this part of Kalinawan

Forest in my life. The realization was so stark that I almost lost my breath again.

"Ligaya is counting on you," I told myself sharply. "You can't give up now."

As I walked through the gray half-light before the dawn, each tree and rock looked exactly like the one before it. This forest was more massive than I'd imagined. I didn't know how I could hope to find any trace of my sister.

And losing my way wasn't even my biggest worry. Every few steps, I heard a cry or howl, neither of which sounded like any normal, friendly creature I'd ever heard. After the fire spirits, I wasn't so sure I wanted to investigate, so I kept walking.

I shivered. Then I sniffled. On top of everything, this rain was no doubt going to give me a cold.

After hours of trudging through the damp and dark, even the scolding my mother would have in store for me when she found out I'd escaped was preferable to this.

Suddenly, I heard a high-pitched shriek through the leaves.

I backed against a tree, heart pounding, even though it sounded like it came from a good distance away.

Swordmaster Pai's words floated into my mind unbidden. *Wicked, heartless monsters teem in the forests . . .*

Just when I thought the trees had gone quiet again, another scream tore through the air. It was closer this time. And unlike the first shriek, it sounded like a person.

My eyes narrowed. *In fact, it sounds familiar . . .*

The foliage right beside me thrashed violently as something ran through it. Breathing hard, I pointed my blade to meet the threat.

A messy-haired boy burst out of the shrubs with a water bakunawa flying fast on his heels. When he saw me, he yelped.

I lowered my sword. "Kiri?"

My friend slowly took his hands away from his face. "Tani! It's you!" After a moment of shock, Kiri hugged me tightly. I squeezed him back, grateful beyond words to see another friendly human in this forest. Luntian coiled around both our shoulders, the bakunawa purring happily as he attuned to his master's excitement.

I stepped away, still wary. "Was that you who screamed earlier?"

"No. Yes. Well, not the first time. That was . . ." Kiri trailed off, his face pale. I noticed that Luntian's scales had lost their emerald luster—a sure sign of anxiety.

"Are you out here alone?" I asked, moments before a familiar figure crashed through the leaves.

"Next time," Bato gasped, swiping angrily at his bangs stuck to his forehead, "maybe *don't* run away like a terrified mouse."

Behind him, Iska hissed venomously, all her sharp fins fanning out. If fire bakunawa hated one thing in the world, it was being soaked in water.

Kiri shrank back, and I moved protectively in front of

him, feeling the resentment toward my rival kindle in my stomach. Swordmaster Pai's golden rule of combat had been drilled into us from the beginning—*never leave a comrade behind*—but this was Kiri's first mission.

I glared at Bato. "Didn't you say you could take on thirty tikbalang single-handedly? Maybe Kiri left because he didn't want to steal your glory."

Bato squinted at me. I was sure I looked like a forest creature drenched with rain and covered in dirt and leaves.

"Tani?" he said incredulously. "What are you doing here?"

I drew myself up. "I'm here to rescue my sister."

Bato gave a choking laugh. "Really? You? You're the one who lost her to begin with!"

Though I hated to admit it, I completely deserved his contempt. Ligaya was missing because of me. "That's why I'm doing all I can to get her back."

Bato's mocking smile faded when he saw my expression.

"Does Swordmaster Pai even know you're here?" I asked.

"No," Bato said quickly. Despite his haughtiness, his eyes betrayed a flash of guilt. "He thought I wasn't strong enough to save the princess. So I came here by myself to prove him wrong."

Judging by how pale Kiri was, I got the sense my friend completely agreed with Swordmaster Pai. I suspected the only reason he'd come along in the first place was to convince Bato to change his mind.

"Look, we can argue later," I said, ignoring Bato's scowl. "Now, what were you running from?"

Bato flushed in indignation as if the very thought of running away was beneath him. But then the monstrous shriek pierced through the air again.

It sounded close . . . too close.

"It's a manananggal," Kiri whispered.

The blood in my veins turned to ice. A manananggal was a flying, humanoid ghoul that could split itself in half. While its upper half flew off in search of prey, its legs remained standing on the ground.

My father, Datu Dakila, had been killed fighting a group of those. I couldn't believe that a manananggal was actually *here*—then I remembered I wasn't safely behind the walls of the village anymore. I was in the heart of the forest.

"We were quiet enough that it didn't see us. Well, at least *I* was," Bato said before glaring at Kiri, "while *he* lumbered around like a water buffalo with its legs on backward."

"Hey!" Kiri protested.

I elbowed my friend in the ribs, urging him to be quiet as the sound of flapping wings and a faint smell of sulfur drifted through the trees.

"What were you thinking, coming here? You'll be a creature's snack before sunrise," I hissed. Never mind that I had entered the forest by myself. "Come on, we need to get away from here. *Now.*"

"We?" Bato demanded. "Since when was there a 'we'? I can fight my way through this forest and rescue Princess Ligaya all on my own!"

"Bato," I groaned. "Now is not the time."

Luntian circled around us, shivering and flicking his tail. Bato pushed the restless bakunawa aside and stomped up to me.

"You can't tell me what to do," he said. "Unlike you, Tanikala, I won the trial honestly. I'm a *real* Serpent Rider—I should've been the one born to save the moon. Now I will be the hero."

The worst thing was that Bato was entirely right. All I ever wanted was a bakunawa, to fulfill my father's legacy and become the warrior my people needed. But what did it really matter, if I had to cheat to get there? Was any legacy worth lying for—or losing a sister for?

"All right then," I said, turning away. "Please bring my sister back, since I know I already failed her." I kicked a rock.

Bato blinked, my reply obviously catching him by surprise. His lip curled as he walked away.

After our heated exchange, the only sound was water dripping from the leaves.

I paused. The whole forest had gone deathly quiet.

Luntian was moving erratically now, like he wanted to either fight or flee.

Bato hesitated, his hand going to his dagger. Shrugging, he continued on to show he was unfazed.

Then the manananggal exploded through the trees.

Chapter 11

Kiri screamed.

Instinctively, I pushed him behind me and drew my kampilan. I gripped the hilt tighter in a futile effort to stop my hands from shaking.

Bato scrambled backward, gasping at the horrifying creature looming above.

The manananggal's needlelike teeth gleamed beneath red eyes and a fall of lank hair. The creature looked like a human woman . . . except its lower half was missing. The monster's powerful, batlike wings kept it airborne as black ichor dripped onto the ground from its severed torso.

It was kin to the creature that killed my father.

While Kiri and I stared at the manananggal in stunned terror, Bato chose the sensible option of drawing his swords and lashing out. The manananggal hissed as he cut a deep, bloody line across its arm. It burst forward, clawed hands stretching out to seize Bato by the throat.

Iska opened her jaws, fire blasting from between her fangs and engulfing the manananggal in a blazing fireball. The creature howled as it was consumed by flames—a living, breathing torch. I flinched back from the heat of the blaze.

Kiri pulled out his own dagger with trembling hands. "Luntian," he said.

His bakunawa didn't appear.

"Luntian?"

The green bakunawa peeked out from behind a bush, terrified.

Kiri stomped over and hauled Luntian out into the open. "Come on! Attack it, just like we practiced!"

I waved my arms frantically. "Hang on, I don't think that's such a good—"

Bolstered by his master's resolve, Luntian reared and spat a jet of water straight at the burning manananggal. The fire sizzled out with a hiss of steam. The manananggal—now a skeletal specter of burned hair and skin—shook off the water drops and charged at Bato.

"Seriously?" Bato yelled as the creature arrowed toward him. "You *put it out?*"

Kiri's face paled. He was breathing hard, trying not to dissolve into panic. "Think, think, think . . ."

I ran into the manananggal's path, swinging my father's sword with all my strength. This blade had killed these creatures before. Sure enough, bones snapped beneath the metal as the winged beast was flung into a tree.

The manananggal slumped to the ground, its head lolling.

We all held our breaths. *Is it dead?*

The flicker of hope died as a shaking hand reached toward the rough bark of the tree. Sharp claws dug in deep. Slowly, agonizingly, the creature pulled itself back upright.

Bato breathed out a curse.

I couldn't believe it. This thing was unkillable.

"Quickly," I shouted at Bato. "Tell Iska to burn it!"

"She can't," he snapped back. "That first fireball took most of her strength. With all this rain, it won't come back for a while."

The terrible truth hit me. We were in the middle of the forest, soaked to the bone, facing a creature who wanted to suck every drop of blood from our veins.

Now there was no Swordmaster Pai to protect us if we made a mistake. If we failed now, we couldn't simply get back up, dust ourselves off, and start again.

This wasn't training anymore. This was reality.

Why can't we kill it? I thought furiously. *If the manananggal was a normal creature, it would be worse than dead by now . . .*

Suddenly I was back in our lesson hall, listening as Swordmaster Pai told us stories from his battle days. No matter how big, no matter how strong, every creature had a fatal weakness. And with manananggal, there was only one way to kill them for good . . .

"That's it." I realized. "I've got to find its lower half."

When a manananggal was near death, its upper half would fly back to wherever it had hidden its legs, connect to them, and regenerate its health. The only way to defeat it was to destroy its lower half, preventing it from healing. When sunrise came, the creature would perish in the light.

Iska slithered to Bato's side, hissing, as the mananang-gal took to the air on crooked, burned wings. Even though the bakunawa's magic was extinguished, her fangs were still deadly as knives.

Bato's eyes never left the feral monster. "All right," he said, for once agreeing with me. "Hurry!"

But how was I supposed to find its lower half in this forest? I looked at the fearsome mananangal, ooze drip-ping from its severed torso, and the answer came—all I had to do was follow the trail. Black stains gleamed on the foli-age around me. Leaving Bato and Kiri to deal with the crea-ture, I followed the trail of ooze through the forest until I came to a mighty tree shrouded in vines.

Gingerly, I pushed the vines aside, and gasped—the tree was completely hollow.

If I were a creature who needed to keep my bottom half safe, then I couldn't think of any better hiding place.

Sure enough, the mananangal's hips and legs stood inside the hollow tree like a grotesque statue, half buried in broken branches and leaf litter.

I heard Swordmaster Pai's voice in my mind. *Rub the sev-ered portion with salt, garlic, or charcoal . . .*

I panicked for a moment—how was I going to find salt

or garlic in the forest? And then I felt the jar of charcoal I'd brought thump against my leg.

I untied the lid and grabbed a handful of black dust. I grimaced—the manananggal's legs glistened with ooze. But if I didn't act quickly, the owner of these legs would make Kiri and Bato pay a far dearer price.

Before I could smear the severed monster with charcoal, the vine curtain behind me blew into the hollow, tendrils whipping my back. The manananggal was here. Both of its arms were sliced clean off, with countless other wounds across its mottled, burned skin, but it somehow managed to keep airborne—just barely.

Bato and Iska charged in behind the monster. My rival's face was splattered with dark ichor, and though I had wanted to pound his face in so many times over the years, right now, I fervently hoped that none of it was *his* blood.

"Tani!" Bato yelled. "Watch out!"

The manananggal tucked in its wings and swooped toward me.

For a moment, I stood transfixed by the creature; a perfect image of evil and ferocity.

Then I whirled around and slammed my charcoal-covered hand into the slimy severed limbs. Wincing in disgust, I swiped my palm across the flesh, which began to smoke as if the cooled charcoal was still aflame.

As soon as that was done, I flattened myself to the ground.

The manananggal shrieked and scrabbled frantically as it tried to reattach itself, screaming at the charcoal's burning touch. But with each passing heartbeat, its wings grew weaker, the unnatural strength drained from its body.

I rolled to my feet and ran, not stopping until I barreled straight into Bato. He hardly noticed me, his eyes fixed on the tree.

Dark smoke billowed as the charcoal did its work. Through the haze, a shadow moved.

The manananggal's upper half shot out of the cloud, jaws spread wide, revealing double rows of shattered teeth.

Its last, desperate revenge.

We drew our swords, ready for the final stand.

And then the sun finally broke the horizon. As the rays of golden light hit it, the manananggal's skin cracked like dried leather, disintegrating. The crumbled dust held itself suspended in the air for a single instant, before ash showered us like rain.

I glanced at Bato. He was in such a mess after the fight that he looked like a monster himself. We both did.

To my surprise, he gave me a grudging nod.

The undergrowth behind us rustled. We spun to face the new threat—but it was only Kiri, pulling at a long green tail that had gotten stuck.

"Come on, Luntian!" he panted. "They need us!"

With a hiss of resignation, Luntian uncoiled from the

branch he had wrapped himself around. Kiri—who was still pulling—flew backward and landed in a heap at our feet.

He blinked up at us, dazed. "Oh," Kiri said. "It's . . . finished."

"No thanks to you," Bato muttered.

Seeing the murderous look in his eyes, I tried to defuse the situation. "Hey. We're alive. That's enough to be thankful for, right?"

Bato scowled. It quickly turned into a grimace.

"What's wrong?" I asked. Then I noticed the bleeding cut on his arm.

"Manananggal are poisonous," Kiri offered. "Moving around too much will circulate the toxins in your body, and you might even lose an arm, if not worse . . ."

Kiri faltered as Bato shot him a look that was almost as venomous as the poison in his arm.

"I *know*."

But even Bato couldn't stay angry for long. Now that the energy of the fight had faded, his face paled as he struggled against the pain. There was no way he could walk *anywhere* in that condition.

"Here, let me help." I cut off the bottom of my cloak and wrapped a broad strip around Bato's arm.

Kiri watched us worriedly. "We've been out in this rain all night. We need to make a shelter and rest, *right now*."

Bato swayed on his feet. Iska was at her master's side at

once, letting Bato slump over her back. What he really needed was a healer.

Using our blades, Kiri and I hacked off leaves and branches and assembled them into a crude shelter like Swordmaster Pai had taught us. We hunkered down on the wet branches, our faces as gloomy as the weather. I was so exhausted I didn't even care that the wood was poking into my skin.

Bato slid limply off Iska's back as the bakunawa came into the shelter. I moved over to help, but Iska hissed at me until I moved away.

The only one who seemed unbothered was Luntian, who obviously loved wet weather. Now that the manananggal had been dealt with, the serpent looked far more relaxed as he splashed around in puddles.

I cast the bakunawa an irritated glance. *At least* someone's *happy.*

I heard sticks clacking together and saw Kiri trying to make a fire, but with all the wood soaked through, it was impossible. It would be a long, cold day for us.

"Give up, Kiri. It's not going to work." Exhaustion made the words come out sharper than I intended.

Kiri let the sticks fall with a clatter.

"Just rest," I said, my eyes flickering closed. "We'll need it if we're planning to get home."

Kiri's voice pulled me back awake. "I *am* useless, aren't I?"

"What?"

Kiri looked at me. I was surprised to see the darkness in his expression. "It *was* you, wasn't it?"

My tired brain struggled to understand his odd questions. "What?" I repeated.

"At the trial. I didn't get that statue on my own. You helped me get it."

"I didn't—"

"You were in the balete tree, Tani, with your bakunawa. I saw you."

I scrambled for something to say. "Yes, I *was* in the balete tree, but you got that statue first. You won fair and square, just like Bato."

"I was *going* to grab the statue," Kiri shot back, "and then it just ... *fell* into my hands. Like magic." Before I could speak, he cut me off with a little smile. "You know, if you *really* hadn't helped me get the statue, you wouldn't be trying so hard to defend yourself now."

My face colored. I hadn't thought of that.

Kiri sighed. "Even then, Tani, you *knew* I wasn't good enough. Even when I was so close to the prize, you still didn't believe I could reach it on my own."

Any words I would have said died on my tongue. I felt a different kind of regret punch into me, in the exact same spot it had hit when Ligaya vanished. Kiri was right—I *had* thought he couldn't do it. I hadn't given him the chance to prove himself ...

The only thing I was good at was letting people down.

"I'm sorry, Kiri." I grimaced. I had to say it, but both of us knew the apology didn't really make up for anything.

Just like saying sorry won't bring Ligaya home.

In the tense silence, Bato shivered under the poison's grip. Iska's scales glowed faintly as she coiled around him, trying to keep him warm, but it wasn't doing much to help.

"Maybe if a stronger person had come instead," Kiri said softly, "Bato wouldn't be hurt."

I shook my head. "If anyone's useless here, it's me. It's my fault Ligaya's gone."

We huddled in our cloaks, wet and cold. In that moment, we couldn't have been further from the glorious image of the Serpent Riders we dreamed of being just days ago.

Chapter 12

Who are you?"

I blinked awake, hungry and exhausted. It couldn't have been more than a few hours since I'd gone to sleep.

"Who are you?" The stranger's voice came again, more insistent. The back of my neck prickled. My bruised muscles protested as I sat up, reaching for my sword.

It wasn't there.

Fear shot through me. I *always* kept my sword close by.

Glancing around, I saw about a dozen people fanned out around our shelter, carrying axes and sickles. One man wore the brightly colored clothes of a leader.

The carved wooden jaws of a bakunawa gaped from the sash around his middle—the hilt of my father's kampilan.

Despite my fear, I felt my blood rise. "That's mine."

Some of the strangers, who were clearly farming people by the tools they held, looked surprised. Others broke out into laughter.

Their leader smiled like he was speaking to an insolent child. "My name is Datu Atay," he said. "I apologize for taking your sword without your permission, but with that wild light in your eyes, I fear that half of my people would be skewered by now had I let you keep it."

My face burned. "Well, I know better now, so may I please have it back?"

The silver-haired datu shook his head. "First, I need to know who you three are and why you are here."

I narrowed my eyes, but there wasn't much I could do. Bato was still knocked out from the venom, with Iska by his side hidden in the shadows of the shelter. Luntian—as I'd come to expect from the flighty bakunawa—was nowhere to be seen.

The only ally I had was Kiri. He was currently fast asleep.

"Hey!" I hissed, kicking his foot. "There are strangers here!"

Kiri startled awake. "Huh?"

The foreign villagers laughed.

Leaving Kiri to come to his senses, I decided to tell them the truth. "My name is Tanikala," I grudgingly admitted. "These are my friends, Bato and Kiri. We're from Kalinawan."

"Kalinawan?" asked a wide-eyed woman. "The village of warriors who ride on the backs of serpents?"

"That's ridiculous, Saya," snorted a mean-looking man. Unlike the rest of the villagers, he wore a red cloth tied around his forehead. "Everyone knows Kalinawan is nothing but a children's story."

While a part of me prickled with injured pride, I didn't blame them for not knowing. We in Kalinawan kept to ourselves, growing our own food and making our own tools so that we could focus on training our warriors. I'd never even heard of Datu Atay's village until today.

I began, "We're not a—"

At that moment, one of the strangers accidentally stepped too close to our shelter. Iska appeared in a copper flash, a flame sparking between her jaws.

The villagers flinched back. Several gasps rang out.

I was unable to resist a grin as Iska hissed at the villagers menacingly. "Don't worry," I said. "She won't hurt you if you don't hurt us." *I hope.*

"You three are warriors?" spat the man with the red headband. "You *children*?"

"We are," I said proudly. "The three of us have just killed a manananggal."

To my surprise, the strangers suddenly fell quiet.

"Manananggal?" Datu Atay repeated. "There is only one such monster that we know of. Are you telling me that you killed Aling Sugat, the creature which has terrorized our village for years?"

Our battle-stained appearance must have spoken for itself, because the datu didn't even wait for an answer before he sent the mean-looking man to investigate. The man glared at us suspiciously before disappearing into the forest.

"If Aling Sugat is dead, you three are heroes indeed," Datu

Atay said, handing me back my sword. "This rainy forest is no place for heroes to rest. Please, come to our village."

The chance to have a dry roof over our heads was too good to pass up. But there was something far more important to deal with first.

"Our friend was badly injured by the manananggal," I explained, pointing to Bato. "Please, you have to help him."

"Of course!" said Datu Atay, appearing guilty that he'd overlooked Bato's condition. "Make him a stretcher at once."

It took some time for me and Kiri to convince Iska to allow the villagers near Bato. But once our unconscious companion was safely on the stretcher, we started off toward the village. As it turned out, it wasn't that much further from where we'd set up camp.

The village had about two dozen wooden houses clustered together. I was surprised to see several black wild pigs lazing in the puddles left by the rain. Some of them snorted at the sight of Iska, but most just rolled over and paid the bakunawa no mind.

I glanced at Kiri. He was just as wide-eyed as I was.

We weren't the only ones in awe. Villagers paused their daily tasks to regard us with fascination. Most of all, their eyes were drawn to Iska, who looked magnificent with her burning eyes and gleaming copper scales. Surrounded by admiring glances, I drew myself up a little straighter. I felt like a hero.

"Datu," one of the villagers called, dropping the bolo knife he'd been using to chop wood. His eyes narrowed. "Who are these strangers?"

"These *strangers* have just saved all our lives," Datu Atay replied. "Aling Sugat, the manananggal, has been slain."

Beside the wood chopper, a woman gasped. "No! These children? That cannot be."

The man wearing the red headband returned from his search of the forest. With tight lips, he handed a sack to Datu Atay. As soon as the datu upended the sack, ash plumed into the air, burned bones clattering to the ground.

A stunned silence fell.

"Quickly!" the woman cried. "Get everything ready; we must have a feast!"

A feast? So many bizarre things had happened that I only now remembered how hungry I was. My mouth watered as the woman rattled off a long list of food. Even though they'd never heard of us and we'd never heard of them, I couldn't have been happier that our ideas of a feast were exactly the same.

"That's nowhere near enough!" someone cried. "We haven't had a feast in ages. Now that Aling Sugat is gone, we can feast all we want!"

Already, pots of sweet sticky rice, purple yams, and other delicacies were boiling, sending a delicious aroma into the air. My stomach growled, but I pushed down my hunger. Both of us would be dead if it weren't for Bato—food was nowhere near as important as a friend's life hanging in the balance.

"Wait!" I pointed to Bato lying on the stretcher. "Our friend is infected with the manananggal's poison. You can repay us by helping him."

"Take him to Babaylan Awit at once," Datu Atay commanded.

The stretcher bearers set off through the milling people, heading for a house whose doorframe was hung with strings of tiny bells, beads, and shells.

Kiri and I followed the villagers into the small house. With all of us inside, it was a tight squeeze.

"What's going on here?" came a snappy voice. "Why are there so many people? Can't a babaylan work in peace?"

The two villagers hurriedly but gently put Bato's stretcher on the floor. They backed out of the babaylan's house so quickly, it was like his words had been sharper than a whip.

The room was wreathed in shadow, the only illumination coming from embers of charcoal in a shallow clay pot. Plants and tools glinted in the flickering light. I wasn't scared. If I closed my eyes, I could almost believe I was back in Babaylan Kalan-ya's house.

The irritated voice—which I assumed belonged to Babaylan Awit—brought me back to the present. "Why are there still people in here!"

"We are very sorry, Babaylan," Kiri said hastily. "We were just wondering if you could heal our friend. He got poisoned by the manananggal, and—"

"I know!" Babaylan Awit interrupted. "Why else would you be in here if you didn't need my help?"

Kiri sat back, looking more confused than offended.

"Don't just sit there like a half-baked sweet potato! Pass me that jar behind you."

Kiri sprang into motion in such a hurry that he almost dropped the jar. I studied the babaylan as he peered inside the container.

Babaylan Awit's hair was white as summer clouds, hanging down his back and pooling around him where he sat cross-legged on the floor. Feathers, beads, and metal rings were knotted into the strands. In the firelight, his face was as lined and cragged as the bark of a balete tree.

The old man withdrew his fingers from the jar covered in a pale, bitter-smelling ointment. He looked over the unconscious Bato with a critical eye.

"You there." He glanced at me. "We have to wash all this dirt and blood off his arm. Use that bowl to fetch water from the well. It's just outside."

As I moved off to do his bidding, I saw sadness flicker over Kiri's face. No doubt he was thinking that if Luntian was here, the water bakunawa could have cleaned Bato's wound in a pinch—but the serpent hadn't shown up since we'd left the forest.

Well, either that, or Luntian's unpredictable powers would have soaked us all in a watery explosion.

Once I had the water, I did my best to wash the grime off Bato's arm. The injury looked gruesome, but Bato didn't even stir. Babaylan Awit smeared a generous amount of the ointment onto the wound. To my amazement, the cream quickly turned black.

"It's drawing the poison out," the old babaylan explained.

"That's incredible," I said. "Is it magic?"

Babaylan Awit gave a gap-toothed grin. "It's a type of magic, yes." He wiped off the black ointment with a cloth and applied a new layer. "The magic entrusted to the babaylan and their healing arts. But the most powerful magic— the ability to call upon the forces of nature itself—hasn't been gifted to humans since the last Mahika disappeared."

Kiri cast me a shifty glance. My cheeks burned in shame as I remembered Mutya and the dark magic she'd used to make a shadow bakunawa. The magic had flown to her as easily as a mother calling a child.

"Is something wrong?" Babaylan Awit asked.

"Uh," I faltered, aware my face was still red. "Babaylan, is there any other way for a human to use magic?"

The old man's smile faded. "No. There is no other way."

A silence settled over the hut, which Babaylan Awit seemed perfectly happy about. He washed his hands before tidying up his utensils and jars.

After a while, he looked up sharply. "What are you two still doing here? Haven't you got better things to do than watch an old man do his work?"

Kiri and I leaped to our feet. "Yes, of course," I stammered. "Sorry. And thank you."

I cast one last hesitant look at Bato.

Babaylan Awit chuckled. "Don't worry. This young warrior is in good hands. Enjoy your celebratory feast. Oh," he added, "one more thing. Please be careful. Sometimes the scariest monsters hide beneath the friendliest skins."

I blinked in surprise. That was an odd way to say farewell. But when the old man's face grew impatient again, I decided not to press it and ducked outside with Kiri.

The setting sun had painted the sky in streaks of burning orange. Smoke from cooking fires plumed into the sky, carrying the scent of roasted meat. On top of a long table covered with banana leaves sat mounds of rice, roasted meat slathered in rich, dark sauce, and stewed vegetables. People of all ages gathered around the table, chattering excitedly.

Kiri's eyes shone with enthusiasm. "Finally," he groaned. "I'm *starving.*"

I was too, but before making my way down, I glanced back at Iska. The copper bakunawa looped restlessly around Babaylan Awit's hut, trying to peer through the windows. A pang of sympathy ran through me. Because Iska had hatched so early, her bond with Bato was stronger than most of the others'—no doubt she was feeling every inch of her master's pain.

"Don't worry," I told the serpent. "Bato will be fine."

Iska hissed and bared her fangs at me. *All right,* I thought. *I'll leave you alone.*

Outside, I searched the crowd for Datu Atay. If Mutya had taken Ligaya through the forest, maybe some of the villagers had seen them.

But the datu was nowhere to be seen among those preparing the feast. As Kiri and I kept searching, I suddenly recognized his voice coming from inside a house with intricate carvings on the eaves—it was probably the datu's own house. There was also another voice that sounded vaguely familiar, but they spoke so softly I couldn't make out the words.

Then the door abruptly swung open to reveal Datu Atay himself. Guiltily, we jumped back from the windows, but I couldn't see past him to find out who he'd been talking to. For some reason, he still carried the empty sack that had contained the manananggal's ashes.

Datu Atay looked surprised to see us, but as the rest of the villagers took notice of us standing there, he raised his voice. "Behold, our young heroes!"

I waved as everyone cheered and clapped. The datu ducked back inside before emerging with two cups of coconut juice, which he held out for us.

"Wow," Kiri said after taking a sip. "You guys grow really good coconuts out here. The ones back home don't taste anywhere near as sweet."

The datu smiled proudly. "Don't worry, we've got plenty more of it."

We wandered over to the food table and started digging in, using our hands. I almost melted at how delicious it all was.

"So, you three are Serpent Riders from Kalinawan?" Datu Atay asked after a while.

I colored. "Well, only Bato and Kiri are. Not me."

He frowned. "But you only have one bakunawa, the copper one."

It was Kiri's turn to blush. "My bakunawa is . . . well, he . . . he ran away."

"Even so, defeating a manananggal as powerful as Aling Sugat was no small feat," the datu said. "The creature was a blight upon our village for years, stealing our pigs and attacking our children. Unlike Kalinawan, we are not a village of warriors, so we owe you our deepest thanks."

I shifted uncomfortably at the praise. "We have to thank you too, for taking us to Babaylan Awit. I don't know where Bato would be right now if he hadn't seen a proper healer."

"Ah, the babaylan." The man's face darkened. "My father is a good enough healer, but I worry that he doesn't have the village's best interests at heart."

That was strange—how could Babaylan Awit not care for his village if he had just healed Bato, a stranger? Before I could ask Datu Atay what he meant, he held up a clay pitcher. "More coconut juice?"

Kiri glanced around as our cups were refilled. "Isn't anyone else having any?"

"We only make this drink on special occasions—and of course, the honor of tasting it is solely reserved for our honored guests." Datu Atay smiled. It might have been my imagination, but his smile seemed forced somehow.

People began to dance in a circle, beating metal drums in a chiming rhythm as those watching clapped along. While

Datu Atay was distracted by the dance, I locked eyes with Kiri and shook my head. We tipped out our drinks behind our backs. Something about this celebration felt off, and I only wanted to eat what everyone else was having.

I thought all the villagers were having a great time—until I caught sight of the man with the red cloth around his head, glowering at the feast with his face like thunder.

But he slipped out of my mind as I decided that now was the perfect time to ask the datu if he'd seen Ligaya.

"Datu Atay, we came through the forest because we're looking for my sister. She was kidnapped from Kalinawan by a sly magician." I swallowed. "Have you seen her?"

The man's brows creased. "I'm sorry, but I haven't."

Just as my heart began to sink, he pointed toward the horizon, where a cloud-capped mountain speared into the sky.

"If a magician took your sister, I can't think of any other place she might have been taken but there. We call it Mount Mahiwaga. My father tells me it's the home of the engkanto, creatures infused with magical powers gifted by the Spirits themselves. With those powers, they could help you—but they'll more likely curse you."

He looked at us warningly. "It's also the place where the Mahika used to live, if you believe the stories."

The longer I gazed at the mountain, the more I imagined I could *see* things, like lights dancing along the slopes. I shook my head and the lights vanished.

The celebration continued until the sun sank below the edge of the world, replaced by glittering stars that wheeled across the charcoal sky. The cooking fires burned down to embers, and the long table was cleared of food so that not even a single scrap was wasted.

"You can stay in my house for the night," Datu Atay offered. "Until your friend gets better."

"Thank you, Datu." I smiled. "For the feast. For everything."

When Kiri and I reached Datu Atay's house, there was no sign of the person he'd been speaking with earlier. I collapsed onto a sleeping mat, completely drained. Homesickness washed over me at how similar everything was to my own home in Kalinawan. I could almost imagine Ligaya was weaving in the next room.

A hand squeezed mine.

"Don't worry, Tani," Kiri said from his sleeping mat. "We'll find Ligaya. Even if we have to search the entire mountain."

I swallowed the lump in my throat. Even after all that had happened, Kiri was still my friend—had *always* been my friend. That loyalty was its own kind of courage.

"You *are* brave, Kiri," I said. "Don't believe anyone who tells you you're not. Even me."

A silence fell as Kiri weighed up my words. Finally, he whispered, "Luntian?"

He didn't need to speak any louder, because his call through their bond would have been louder than a shout. We waited, but the green bakunawa didn't appear.

Kiri let out a breath. "He's not far away." I wasn't sure if

Kiri was trying to convince me or himself. "I can sense him waiting at the edge of my mind. He hears me, but he doesn't want to come." His voice faltered. "Something about this village terrifies Luntian . . . but I don't know what it is."

Kiri's words sounded faintly ominous, and despite the warm night, a chill shivered along my skin.

The silence deepened. Just when I was sure that Kiri had fallen asleep, his voice drifted through the gloom once more.

"You know, Luntian and I made a promise to each other, the day we won the trial. We promised that we would never leave each other behind. Even in the face of impossible odds, if one of us is in trouble, the other will come to save him no matter what."

"Do you think Luntian will keep his promise?" I found myself asking.

"I know he will," Kiri answered. Then he went on, in a voice almost too quiet for me to hear. "He has to."

I didn't have anything more to say. Soon the night was filled with the sound of Kiri's breathing as he fell asleep.

I rolled over and looked at my bakunawa egg wrapped in my sash on the floor. Its black shell would have been invisible in the night had it not been for the flecks of gold.

I sighed. "Now would be a perfect time to hatch, you know. Ligaya needs you."

I wondered if the little bakunawa curled inside could hear me.

My thoughts drifted to other things. If Babaylan Awit was right about human magic disappearing with the last

Mahika, then the conclusion was clear—Ligaya had been kidnapped by the Mahika herself.

It felt impossible since the Mahika disappeared long ago and should have been an old woman now. More unbelievable was that our legendary hero and protector had betrayed us by taking Ligaya captive. But I had seen Mutya use nature magic with my own eyes. She couldn't possibly be anyone else.

Now, Ligaya was in more danger than any of us had imagined. And as far as I could tell, we were the only ones who knew where she was.

I didn't know how I could possibly fight someone who was strong enough to banish Great Bakunawa. Then I remembered, for all her magic, even the Mahika couldn't destroy the Moon Eater forever. The only person who could do that was *me*. I was stronger than Mutya, and that meant she could be defeated.

Most of all, Ligaya was my sister. And nothing—not even the most powerful magician in the land—could stop me from finding her.

Chapter 13

A sharp, piping noise startled me awake. I cracked my eyelids open, feeling a thousand drums pound inside my skull.

Sitting up, I felt a wave of nausea roll through me. I would've thought that after a belly full of food and a few hours of rest, I'd be feeling a lot better than this . . .

Then a flash of light outside bathed the room in molten orange.

Fire. Something's on fire.

Stunned, I caught a glimpse of rainbow feathers as something flew through the window and into the room. The creature had a pair of swooping wings and a long, elegant tail. *Those feathers look exactly like the one I saw on Ligaya's loom . . .*

"Hey!" Kiri spluttered awake as the bird hopped on top of him. I tried to get a better look at it, but my eyes refused to focus.

What is wrong with me?

The rainbow bird gave a high, piping whistle. It hopped from foot to foot, restless. Urgent.

I squinted. "Why are you here?"

As the bird flew to the window, I struggled to stand. The world swayed dizzyingly—or maybe it was me who had unsteady feet. I felt sick to my stomach. Even through the fog in my mind, my chest twisted as realization hit me.

"Poison," Kiri confirmed with a grimace, his speech slurred. "It must have been . . . the coconut juice. Datu Atay tricked us."

Fear shot through me. Before we could dwell on the datu's betrayal, a loud roar outside sent us stumbling to the window. There was another bright flash and a thunderous *whoosh* as fire blazed into the night, sending villagers staggering away.

Iska.

"What are they doing?" Kiri whispered, leaning against the wall.

In the firelight, I saw coils of thick rope and sharp blades gleaming in the villagers' hands.

I shuddered, remembering Babaylan Awit's ominous words. *Sometimes the scariest monsters hide beneath the friendliest skins . . .*

We trusted Datu Atay so easily, with his welcoming personality and easy smile. Had Babaylan Awit known that the datu would betray us? Why had he helped Bato at all? Why didn't he warn us directly?

"We have to . . . do something *now*, Kiri." With fumbling

fingers, I grabbed my sword. But before I could draw the blade, my stomach lurched and I doubled over.

"Do *what*?" Kiri shouted hoarsely. "We can . . . barely . . . even stand!"

I shook my head, but it only made the nausea worse. "We don't have a choice. There's no . . . telling what Datu Atay will do to us once he . . . discovers we're awake. Bato and Iska are counting on us."

And so is my sister.

I staggered to the door, almost falling down the steps as it swung open. Then a wicked laugh filtered out of the shadows.

"Look who's just woken up." My heart shot into my throat as a man—the one with the red headband—blocked my path. He waved a bolo knife at me menacingly. "Don't interfere with the datu's business, kid."

I took a deep breath, fighting down a tide of panic.

"You *traitors*." I leveled my own sword at his chest, hoping he didn't notice how much my hands were shaking. "We did nothing to hurt you—we *helped* you by killing the manananggal!"

The man stepped closer. "That's true, but you can help us even more by standing aside and letting us have your copper bakunawa, nice and simple. We don't want anyone to get hurt . . . much." With a wicked laugh, he slashed his knife forward.

I brought my sword up by instinct and our blades clashed together with a metallic ring. But with the poison still running through my veins, I didn't have the strength for a proper block, and the man's knife slipped past my defense to score a red line across my arm.

I fell back with a gasp. My enemy advanced, his lips stretched in a leering grin.

A shape blurred above me as Kiri launched himself at the villager. My friend tried to stab down with his knife, but the man shook him off easily.

The rainbow bird screeched as it swooped down from the sky and barreled into our attacker. The villager swatted wildly with his hands, trying to fend it off, but the bird flew back out of reach before diving down and raking the man's face with its talons. He dropped his knife, staggering away, his face a bloody ruin.

I heard a furious roar somewhere up ahead. *Iska.*

Rolling to my feet, I grabbed my sword. "Come on, Kiri! Let's go!"

I sprinted to where the mob of villagers held Iska captive. The world still tipped around me, but the brisk night wind combined with the rush of battle helped fight off the effects of the weak coconut poison. Datu Atay clearly hadn't considered that Iska was too proud to let herself be captured so easily.

But even the fearsome strength of the bakunawa had its limits. By now, the villagers had managed to bind Iska's jaws with thick rope, preventing her from breathing fire. Embers sparked between the bakunawa's teeth as she tried in vain to break free. More ropes crisscrossed her body. She struggled, but was helpless with so many people holding her down.

With a battle cry, I swung my sword into the crowd of people, sending two of them sprawling. Kiri exchanged blows with another villager, their fluid motions making them look like dancers. My friend fought as well as he could, but he was quickly losing ground.

My blade flashed as I leaped toward them, knocking the knife out of the villager's grasp. The man took one look at his empty hands and fled.

"We have to free Iska," Kiri gasped. "Now's our chance."

I nodded breathlessly. Freeing the bakunawa was the only way we could win—once Iska started spitting fire again, the villagers would be overpowered and forced to let us go.

We ran toward the captive bakunawa, who was thrashing so powerfully against her bonds that it was taking all the remaining villagers to hold her down.

I couldn't help but smile at the sight. *Only the Serpent Riders of Kalinawan are worthy of befriending a bakunawa.*

"I'll cover you," I told Kiri, hefting my sword. "You cut the ropes."

At that moment, I heard an evil laugh from behind me.

"Not so fast, Serpent Warriors."

I whirled around to see Datu Atay step out of the shadows. His shirt and cloak were gone, revealing muscular shoulders swirling with fierce tattoos.

No longer was he the kindly leader who had given us

food and shelter. The man before us was a coldhearted traitor.

"You liar," I said, hot anger blazing through me. "We trusted you to keep us safe!"

"And I would have protected you and your friends with my life," the datu replied calmly. "But your fiery serpent companion is a different matter . . ."

I gritted my teeth. "What does Iska matter to you? She doesn't deserve to die. *Nobody* does."

Darkness stole over the datu's face. "I would never dream of harming such a magnificent creature. Simply put, I have been promised something that I couldn't pass up in exchange for the serpent."

To prove his point, he reached into his sash and pulled out a smooth, pale-colored object.

I sucked in a breath. In his hand was Babaylan Kalan-ya's blue cone shell—the magical talisman I'd stolen from the village, the talisman whose power was able to hold back a berberoka.

The datu smiled at my bewildered expression. "Before the feast, I met a traveler who showed me this ordinary-looking shell. She said it was enchanted to repel monsters. I was doubtful at first, until she told me to retrieve Aling Sugat's ashes and bring them back to her. I couldn't believe my eyes—even though the manananggal was long dead, I couldn't get the ashes anywhere near the shell. I was held back by an invisible barrier."

Now I knew why the person Datu Atay had been

speaking to sounded so familiar. Only one person could have possibly given him the blue cone shell.

"If I captured the bakunawa for her," the datu went on, "she told me I could keep the talisman. With this charm, my people will never have to fear monsters like Aling Sugat again. We will be able to tend our fields, to farm our animals, without being attacked." He paused. "Strange, though, she mentioned there would be *two* serpents . . ."

The datu and his people had made a deal with Mutya to capture our bakunawa and stop us before we could rescue Ligaya. My stomach roiled at the thought of how easily I'd let myself believe that he was going to keep us safe.

His gaze softened for the briefest moment. "I have to put my people first—even if it means ending you."

The datu advanced, drawing his own blade, its edge curved and deadly like the talon of some terrible beast.

Even though I wasn't a true Serpent Rider, I wouldn't go down without a fight, and I held my sword out protectively.

Suddenly, a bony hand latched around Datu Atay's arm, holding him fast.

"Don't hurt them," Babaylan Awit said, a quaver in his thin voice.

Datu Atay blinked down at the old healer, surprised, before he shook the babaylan's hand off like an annoying mosquito.

"Don't interfere with this, Father," the datu growled, his brows drawn in anger. "I'm doing this for our village."

Instead of obeying, Babaylan Awit moved to stand in

front of me and Kiri. Though his body was frail, the determination in his cloudy eyes was stronger than iron.

"Don't hurt them," he repeated.

The datu was struck speechless as if he couldn't believe that the village babaylan—his own father, no less—would defy him like this. His face settled into the scowl of a man betrayed.

"Don't you understand, old man? If we can't grow some crops soon, then all of us will starve." A menacing gleam entered the datu's eye as he pointed his sword at his father's chest. "If you don't get out of my way . . . then I have no choice but to cut you down as well."

For the first time, I saw a flicker of fear in Babaylan Awit's eyes. I lunged forward, but Datu Atay easily knocked my sword out of my grasp.

As the echo of ringing metal faded, the rainbow bird dived down from the sky, talons outstretched toward Datu Atay's head.

"Watch out!" Kiri yelled.

His warning wasn't for the datu but for the bird, which soared away just in time as the man swung his blade overhead.

And then, to my surprise, it began to sing.

The song was soft and low, just on the edge of hearing. Sorrowful and aching, like a lament for the lost, each note filled with such deep longing that it brought tears to my eyes.

I was utterly transfixed. Spellbound. Datu Atay's weapon

fell from his grasp and thumped to the ground. A dark gray patch appeared on his sword arm, slowly spreading out.

What is happening to him?

Babaylan Awit snapped out of the trance. "Cover your ears!" he shouted hoarsely at the datu, "or the Adarna's song will turn you to stone!"

The villagers surrounding the trapped bakunawa realized what was happening. Frantic with terror, a few had the sense to clap their hands over their ears and flee, but those who hadn't heard Babaylan Awit's warning slowly turned into statues of dark rock, frozen in the final moments of their fear.

I braced myself for the Adarna's spell to take hold of me. To my shock, nothing happened, even though I'd already heard the song. Kiri and the babaylan weren't covering their ears either, and though they looked terrified, they were unharmed.

Everyone else was changing into stone. But why weren't we?

Numb with horror, I lay shaking on the ground. Before I could even think about what to do next, a shadow fell over me.

Datu Atay.

How was he still moving? Hadn't he turned to stone? Then I saw the answer: he'd stuffed handfuls of mud into his ears to block out the song.

Rage and desolation swept his face as he stared at the doomed villagers.

"Now," he roared, "my choice is clear. You all must die!"

Icy fear gripped my spine. I glanced helplessly at my kampilan, far out of reach.

"My son, is this what you have become?" Babaylan Awit's eyes filled with tears.

But Datu Atay didn't hear him, or at least pretended not to. He raised his sword, the curved blade brighter than the moon.

I didn't flinch as the sword arced down.

Chapter 14

If this truly was the end, at least I knew I had been trying to bring my sister home.

But to my shock, the sword stopped just fingerbreadths from my skull.

I looked up to see a glittering green coil wrapped around the datu's muscular arm, keeping the blade from falling any further.

Luntian!

The datu struggled against the bakunawa's grip, but Luntian didn't let go. The serpent opened his jaws and spat a jet of water right at Datu Atay's head.

I flinched as droplets splattered my skin. The datu reeled back, mud dripping down his face where it had been washed out of his ears. His face was a mask of utter disbelief as Luntian released his arm, hissing venomously.

As the Adarna sang on, patches of the datu's skin began to solidify into stone, like a sculpture taking form.

Frantically, Datu Atay lifted the blue shell, hoping it would stop the Adarna's magic—but nothing happened.

"Cover your ears!" Babaylan Awit cried. "Please, my son."

But the datu didn't move. Stone crept across his body.

Instead of saving himself from the deadly song, the datu slowly walked toward the villagers who had already been turned to stone.

"Please . . . ," Babaylan Awit begged.

Then the datu couldn't take a step further—his legs had changed into solid rock. Painfully, he reached toward the nearest stone person, as if his touch alone could break the spell.

Then the magic overcame him, and he fell still. The transformation was complete. He looked eerie, formed in rock, like his features had been carved by a master sculptor. Still cradled in his hand was the blue cone shell trapped in the stone cage of his fingers.

Perched upon a nearby rooftop, the Adarna ceased its song of death.

Babaylan Awit ran toward his son with a choking sob. Kiri leaped to his feet, stunned, as an excited Luntian barreled into him.

"You came back!" Kiri said, glowing with happiness. "I *knew* you wouldn't abandon us."

"Thank you," I told the green bakunawa. "You just saved our lives."

Our relieved smiles faded as Babaylan Awit's desolate wail pierced the air. We knew that even the babaylan's healing knowledge could do nothing to bring the villagers back.

"You must go," he told us weakly. "The villagers who escaped will be back soon. They will be angry."

I moved closer and laid a hand on his thin shoulder. I wanted to say something comforting, but no words would ever be enough.

I knew all too well what it was like to lose family.

But there were too many questions swirling inside me. "When you healed Bato, you warned us that we'd be betrayed," I said. "Why?"

Darkness clouded the old man's gaze. "It is a babaylan's job to heal and protect. When you three arrived with your serpent, I thought my son would do something reckless like this. It was wrong for me to just let you walk into a trap."

Kiri was still confused. "But you defended us when Datu Atay was about to kill us. That was incredibly brave, but why would you risk your life like that?"

Babaylan Awit glanced at Iska, who he had already cut free with his small knife. She looked mostly unscathed, fins rippling as she regarded the old man curiously.

"Have you heard the story of Great Bakunawa?" Babaylan Awit asked.

His question took me by surprise. "Of course," I said. "The mighty Serpent who swallowed six of the seven moons, banished by the Mahika to the bottom of the sea."

"Your village keeps its stories well," he said. "My people have forgotten the legends because they refuse to listen. Like how they forgot the story of the Adarna, the bird that sings the truth of what lies in human hearts. The Adarna saw the depths of their greed and selfishness, and so its song turned them into what they truly were—beings of cold stone."

He sighed. "The fate that befell our village tonight was terrible enough, but a worse end awaits us if Great Bakunawa isn't stopped."

I blinked. "Great Bakunawa is returning? Now?"

Babaylan Awit gestured at the petrified villagers, then at the Adarna. "All of this is not coincidence. Magic is stirring in the air, and I have seen within the smoke that this will only get worse. The Mahika, our only protector, has abandoned us—and without her, the future of our people looks direr than ever."

The old man looked at us appraisingly. "The Moon Eater's return is what you've been training for, is it not?"

That was true—the Serpent Riders *did* learn to command Great Bakunawa's children so that we'd have a way to fight her when she came back to devour the final moon, but I couldn't believe it was going to happen *now*. I didn't like where Babaylan Awit was heading, but if the stories had been wrong about the Mahika's intentions, then perhaps they were also wrong about the timing of Great Bakunawa's return. The only problem was, *I* was supposed to protect the moon, and my bakunawa hadn't even hatched yet.

Babaylan Awit looked me in the eye, and I got the unsettling feeling that he was staring straight through me. "Only you, the Serpent Riders, have any chance at stopping the disaster that will befall our world."

Throat dry, I glanced at Kiri, who was just as speechless as I was.

There was a flicker of movement as a figure appeared in the doorway of the healer's hut. My hand automatically went to the hilt of my sword . . . then my mouth dropped open.

Bato leaned against the doorframe, wearing his usual cocky grin. He was paler and had a white bandage wrapped around his arm, but I wouldn't have otherwise been able to tell he'd been injured at all.

"Hey," he called out. "You got into a fight without me? And you two runts actually *won*?"

I tried to think of a smart reply, but nothing came. "You're healed," I said in amazement.

The ghost of a smile flickered across Babaylan Awit's face—the briefest flash of his old self. "You insult my skill. Of *course* your friend is better."

Kiri ran to Bato and hugged him tightly.

"Ow," Bato said, but he was so surprised he didn't even try to push Kiri off. I couldn't help but smile, remembering how guilty Kiri felt when our friend had been injured.

I couldn't even believe my *own* thoughts. *Am I actually* happy *that this arrogant fool is walking on his own two feet again?*

Iska shot forward and squeezed her master tight in her copper coils. Happy sparks of flame crackled around her jaws.

"Brave girl," said Bato, his face splitting into a grin. "Nice to see you too."

But once he walked down to meet us, his smile vanished, his mouth agape as he saw the stone statues.

Following his gaze, Babaylan Awit sighed. "The legendary Adarna did not turn my son to stone out of malice. Even you saw how the talisman designed to ward off evil creatures did nothing to quell its song. And none of you were turned to stone. It was protecting you."

The rainbow bird was beautiful and impressive, yet it wielded a weapon far more lethal than any blade. But I tried to see the bird in a new light. Perhaps it *was* Ligaya's friend. Maybe Ligaya was sending a message. Asking us to bring her home.

The bird regarded me with a black, beady eye that gleamed with intelligence.

"The stories say that the Adarna leads travelers to good fortune," I recited. "Follow the Adarna. It will lead the way."

There was a long silence. Our time in this village was over.

Still, I hesitated. Babaylan Awit had been nothing but kind to us, so leaving him amid all this bleakness felt wrong.

"Take these," he said, giving a clay jar to each of us. "It's the ointment I used to cure the poison. It's deadly to monsters; that is why it is so effective. Perhaps you will need more of it on the way."

I nodded, too emotional to speak.

"Don't worry about me," the healer said, sensing my

thoughts. "If the blue cone shell is even half as powerful as my son claimed, then I shouldn't have to fear for my safety."

He glanced forlornly at the talisman, caught in Datu Atay's stone embrace—wondering, perhaps, how his life had been completely devastated in a single night.

"Go to Mount Mahiwaga," the babaylan told us at length. "It is there you will find the answers you seek . . . and perhaps even help me find mine."

"If there is a way to reverse the stone spell," I promised, "then we will find it."

Babaylan Awit only smiled and turned away. The three of us set off toward the mountain, leaving the old man to mourn his lost son.

Chapter 15

The Adarna flew above us, a glittering beacon leading the way to Mount Mahiwaga. I wasn't the only one keeping an eye on it. Even the fiery Iska was wary and subdued, like there was something about the bird she couldn't comprehend.

I didn't blame her. Before a few hours ago, I would never have imagined that birdsong could turn people to stone.

We passed several rice paddies cut into the hillsides like glassy steps. Most were filled with churned mud rather than the fresh green stalks of new rice plants. I understood why Datu Atay was so desperate for the blue cone shell—there was so much fertile land that his people could farm if they didn't have to worry about monsters.

The summer sun was relentless. By the time we reached the edge of the dense forest that covered the mountain, sweat was streaming down my back.

Without hesitation, the Adarna glided beneath the boughs.

I looked at Kiri. Kiri looked at Bato. Bato looked at me.

The Adarna landed on a branch and tilted its head as if asking, *What's the delay?*

I didn't know why, but a dark feeling roiled in my gut. We were *all* afraid. Of a *forest*.

"Can you sense it?" Kiri whispered. "It's like something is watching us."

Surprised, I discovered he was right. An instinct honed by years of training made the hairs rise on the back of my neck. Although I couldn't see them, I *felt* them. Hidden watchers, shrouded in leaves and shadows.

Magic lived here. I knew it in my bones.

Of course, Bato was the first to snap out of it. "Why are we so terrified of these trees?" He scoffed. "Honestly."

Flicking his long hair out of his face, he sauntered into the forest as Iska trailed behind.

Kiri swallowed. "I suppose we have to follow him?"

A part of me wanted to turn back. This journey had been dangerous enough already—surely we should leave it to more experienced Serpent Riders to venture into such uncharted territory. But then I thought of Ligaya, alone. Lost. Afraid. I didn't have another choice.

"My sister's in there," I said. And I'd cut down a whole army to find her if I had to.

I touched my bakunawa egg for luck and strode into the trees. After a long hesitation, Kiri and Luntian followed.

As soon as the shadows fell over me, the searing heat vanished, a cold sweat breaking out on my skin. Faint whispers echoed among the trees.

I heard Kiri say something under his breath.

"What was that?" I asked.

"Tabi-tabi po," Kiri repeated. The phrase meant "please move aside," which Swordmaster Pai always told us to say. It was a gentle warning to any small spirits to move out of our way, for fear we wouldn't see them and accidentally step on them.

"Took you long enough," Bato drawled. Well, at least he was back to his usual self.

The Adarna led us to a set of stone steps carved into the mountain. Beside them was a stone dish with a figurine crouching over it, its weathered features unrecognizable.

"That's an anito." Kiri pointed at the crouching figure. "The dish is for people to leave offerings to it, like we do at home."

According to Ligaya's stories, and our lessons with Swordmaster Pai, the anito were nature spirits who could either bless or harm, depending on how humans treated them. Since it looked as though this dish had been empty for years, I guessed these anito weren't feeling too happy. Instead of taking care of them, people had abandoned them.

I swiped a finger across the dish, coming away with a thick layer of dirt. "Why doesn't anyone come here anymore?"

Kiri brightened like he did whenever Swordmaster Pai asked him a history question. "When the Mahika disappeared, this mountain fell into ruin. The Serpent Riders fought off the monsters that showed up after she left." His face paled suddenly. "Wait, that means . . ."

"Look out!" I yelled. A shadowy hand reached down from the branches above, huge fingers ready to snatch him up. I swung my sword, but the blade sliced nothing but air.

I blinked. The hand was gone. I scanned the trees but found nothing.

Bato snorted. "Jumping at shadows, Tani?"

Scowling, I shoved my sword back into my sash. "Sorry. Let's go."

"Uh . . . ," Kiri began. I glanced over to see him spinning wildly in place as he searched the leaves overhead. "Which way? The Adarna's gone."

"What?"

The Adarna's glittering rainbow feathers should've been easy to spot, but now there was no sign of it. We waited long moments, but our magical guide didn't come back.

"We already knew we needed to come to Mount Mahiwaga to find Ligaya," I said through gritted teeth. "What's the point in leaving us now?"

"There isn't any," Bato spat. "Typical enchanted creature— it tricked us. I should've let Iska eat it when we had the chance." Iska growled in agreement.

The worn stone steps led further up the mountain. "Maybe the Adarna wanted us to find this stairway?" I ventured. "What if it wants us to climb higher?"

Bato shrugged. "Not like we have a choice."

Before long, the steep climb had all three of us out of breath. The grand feast from the village was a distant memory, and I was exhausted. I even felt sorry for Bato, who had barely eaten anything. Still, he forged on stoically without complaint.

Then we all stopped at the same time.

"Now what?" Kiri panted, staring at the ground.

My stomach sank. The forest had grown over the staircase, leaving no clear path ahead.

Bato looked at me. "Any more bright ideas?"

"Be quiet," I growled, refusing to give up. "We *could* keep climbing . . ."

Kiri groaned. "Sorry, Tani, but my feet can't carry the rest of me one step further."

I was about to protest when I saw Iska and Luntian—their usually bright scales had lost their luster. Poor Luntian, a water serpent, looked especially dried-out after the hot climb.

"Okay," I said, relenting. "We'll rest here for a few hours, then decide what to do."

Kiri collapsed onto the step with a sigh of relief. I sat beside him, feeling the tension leave my muscles. It was our first rest since we'd started walking.

The sinking sun gilded the trees with late afternoon light. That was strange—I thought sunset was still hours away. Or had we really been walking that long?

Worse, we were still hopelessly lost. On this gigantic mountain, we'd never find the Mahika without help. The

Adarna was our only hope of finding Ligaya, and it was missing...

Suddenly, shadows swallowed the sunlight. Night had fallen as quickly as if someone had blown out the sun.

"What...," Bato breathed, looking at the sky.

I felt that familiar shiver along the back of my neck. *Magic.*

"Don't worry," I said with a calmness that belied my pounding heart. "Let's find a nice tree to sleep in and keep the snakes off our feet."

Kiri's face whitened. *Probably shouldn't have mentioned the snakes.*

We plodded onward, looking for somewhere to sleep. Kiri hissed through the darkness as he tripped over fallen branches.

"Careful," I said, unable to resist a smile. "You might attract the snakes."

Kiri grumbled. Suddenly, he stopped short, staring back the way we came. He grabbed my shoulders and pointed.

Strange lights winked in and out between the trees. They looked like balls of flickering blue flame, dancing in the air like gigantic fireflies.

Iska and Luntian shrank away from the lights in fear. Bato sucked in a breath.

The floating fires in Kalinawan Forest had tricked me into almost falling to my death. These were much bigger. Much brighter.

And as if things couldn't get any worse, we heard giant

footsteps trudging through the forest, sending tremors through the ground. They stomped steadily closer—*impossibly close.*

A deep, rhythmic sound vibrated through the air. It sounded like . . . laughter.

"Start running," I whispered. "Now."

We turned and fled for our lives. Away from the orbs of flame, away from the eerie laughter. I didn't even know which way was which anymore.

Kiri cried out as he stumbled over a tree root. Even though every instinct was telling me to run, I spun to help him up.

"I think I'm good," he panted out. Beside him, Luntian whimpered.

The words had barely left his mouth when the leaves above us rustled. Then they thrashed together, as if caught in a fierce wind.

A black shape leaped down from the branches, blocking our escape. We could only stare, terrified into utter silence, as the creature rose to its full height.

It was a kapre—a giant. He wore a cloth around his waist, and his black hair hung down his back. In his hands was a club made of a heavy branch snapped right off the tree.

He glowered down at us, his eyes like lightning.

We were trapped.

Chapter 16

Somebody was screaming. It was Kiri. Wait, it was also me. And Bato. All of us were screaming.

I tried to reach my sword, but it was like a spell had trapped me in place. Or maybe I was frozen with fear.

The giant stomped closer. The earth shuddered with each powerful step. He raised his hands above his head . . .

This is it, I thought. My stomach churned.

Kiri's scream trailed off. "Wait," he said. "He's . . . not killing us."

To my surprise, he was right. Instead of crushing us into red sludge, the giant dropped his club and clapped his pallet-sized hands over his ears.

"Owww," he moaned. His voice rumbled like distant thunder. "Why do the littlest humanlings always make the most noise?"

Humanlings? Numbly, I blinked at him, halfway between confused and terrified.

A green streak shot past as Luntian leaped, growling, toward the giant.

"No!" Kiri cried. "Luntian, don't sacrifice yourself for us!"

The green bakunawa slammed into the giant's chest, barely making the big man stumble. Then, to our astonishment, Luntian slithered up the giant's long beard and started licking the kapre's face with his forked tongue.

"Hey!" the kapre laughed, petting the bakunawa with his huge palm. "Tickles!"

Luntian hissed happily as the giant scratched him behind the two fins on his head. I couldn't believe that the bakunawa's tail was actually *wagging*. But Iska surprised us all by floating over to the giant and waiting for her turn to be petted. By the way Bato was looking at her, I'd have thought he hardly recognized the bakunawa at all.

Kiri shot me a bewildered glance. "That was . . . not what I was expecting."

"Very well," the giant rumbled. "If serpent-beast is friend of humanlings, that means humanlings are friends of Mangwawasak."

The giant sighed in exasperation at our still-confused faces. "Me. Mangwawasak. Means 'destroyer.'" He thumped his barrel chest proudly. "But you can call me Mak."

Luntian was flying happy loops around the giant, making Mak laugh. For a creature who was usually a scaredy-cat, Luntian was doing surprisingly well.

"What's up with them?" I asked, watching the bakunawa.

A thoughtful expression crossed Kiri's face. "I can't sense

any fear in Luntian at all. Like he knows the kapre isn't going to harm us."

I seriously doubted that, but before I could make sense of anything, the kapre spoke up. "What humanlings and serpent-beasts doing here?"

"We're just passing through," I said hesitantly. "We didn't mean to disturb you—we just didn't expect it would get dark so quickly."

"Oh," Mak said, looking for all the world like a little child who just played a grand prank on his older sibling. He pointed at himself. "That me. Mak make it nighttime quickly. Mak like the dark."

"Of course it was," Bato muttered.

I should've known. In the stories, kapre were notorious for playing tricks on hapless villagers. One of their favorites was to fool humans into thinking they had lost their way, whether it be in mountain forests, open fields, or even in their own houses.

"If only the Adarna hadn't disappeared," Kiri said, "then we wouldn't have gotten into this mess."

The kapre's huge brow creased. "Adarna," he repeated, pulling something out of his waistband. "You mean this?"

We stared at him, astonished, for between the deep ridges of his palm sat a golden cage with the Adarna trapped inside.

"Yes, that," I said eagerly. I stretched out my hands expectantly before it fully sank in that the Adarna was in a cage.

Before I could reach it, Mak closed his fist around the cage and tucked it back into his waistband. The Adarna barely had time to squawk before its shimmering feathers disappeared from sight.

Bato stood up angrily. "Give us the Adarna, Mak."

The kapre shook his head like a naughty child. "Mak saw humanlings following Adarna. Mak know humans only ever follow creatures when they want to hunt and kill them."

"We're not hunting it!" I said. "We were following it. We need it to find—"

"Silly little bird," Mak cut in, shaking his head at the Adarna. "Always getting mixed up in human problems. First, humanlings leave. Then Mak will set Adarna free when humanlings are far away from here."

Kiri looked frantically between Mak and the Adarna, alarmed. Even though the kapre was way bigger than us, Bato grabbed hold of his swords, looking just on the verge of throttling the life out of the mischievous giant.

The Adarna was our last hope at finding Ligaya. Without it, my sister would be lost forever.

"Mak," I said. "Please let the Adarna go."

Trapped in the cage, the Adarna suddenly let out a series of long, trilling chirps. The kapre tilted his head like he was listening, before a thoughtful expression came over him.

"All right," Mak rumbled. "Mak will set Adarna free— *only* if humanlings help find what Mak lost."

The three of us exchanged glances. So the kapre wanted to make a deal.

"What is it?" I asked.

Mak scratched his hairy tummy, like he was used to something being there that wasn't anymore. "Mak belt," he said glumly.

"That's it?" Kiri was confused. "You want us to find you a belt?"

"*Mak* belt," the kapre emphasized. "Mak turn invisible when Mak put it on. Like this. See?" Mak squeezed his eyes shut. After a few moments, he opened them again. "But you can't see. Because Mak lost belt."

"Oh, great," Bato muttered. "It's a magic belt."

"Mak know where belt is. Dropped in little hole by accident." A wide grin appeared on his face. "So we go find it now!"

Suddenly, Mak leaned forward and picked all of us up in his hands. I kicked frantically, but the giant kept his grip on us as easily as a child holding a collection of dolls. His fingers smelled of tobacco smoke. Iska and Luntian, completely at ease, floated alongside Mak's shoulder.

"Let us go!" Struggling to reach my sword, I remembered Ligaya's stories about kapre, and their inclination for tearing humans limb from limb.

"Wait!" Kiri cried. Mak held us up to his face, scrutinizing us. Kiri blanched but continued rapidly. "We're really tired after walking all day, and besides, it's so dark we might not even *see* your belt in all this forest. Can't—can't we go looking for it tomorrow?"

Mak's brow furrowed. I could tell he really wanted us to go find his belt, but perhaps the long day we'd had was evident on our faces, because the kapre eventually nodded. "Humanling right. We go look tomorrow."

I let out a breath, looking at Kiri. He'd come up with a brilliant idea to stall for time—maybe, during the night, we could find a way to get the Adarna back. Then we'd make our escape while Mak was sleeping . . .

"Humanlings stay in Mak home," the kapre announced.

What? Was I hearing him properly?

"Thanks, but I don't think we—" Bato's protests went unheard as Mak marched through the underbrush with earthshaking steps. To my amazement, the orbs of blue flame scattered among the trees formed into an orderly line, before floating one by one into the bowl of a huge wooden pipe tucked into the kapre's waistband.

The world tilted sideways as Mak climbed up a balete tree using only his legs, finding footholds in the gnarly roots with practiced ease. He paused at the top of the tree.

"Whoa," Kiri breathed.

The whole mountain slope stretched down before us. Datu Atay's village sat on a distant hill, and further down I saw the lights of Kalinawan, cradled by the silent gray sea.

Home.

Then Mak jumped down through the branches.

A scream rose in my throat as we fell through the darkness. Mak hit the ground, bending his knees for the landing as the impact rattled through my bones.

"Whoa," Kiri repeated.

Despite our predicament, we couldn't help but gaze around in rapt wonder. The inside of this balete tree was completely hollow like a cavern, its walls decorated with fabric woven in intricate patterns. The only light came from a glowing blue fire spirit that illuminated several scattered objects—golden bracelets, wooden spinning tops, and scraps of dyed cloth amid a collection of other things that all looked human-made.

I swallowed. Were these trinkets all that remained of people who had been unlucky enough to cross the kapre's path?

"This Mak home," Mak said proudly, setting us down. He noticed me looking at the assortment of objects and frowned. "Humans dump things in forest all the time. Forest not happy. So, Mak pick up pretty things and bring them here."

Whistling to himself, Mak reached inside a hollow between roots and pulled out three mangoes, giving one to each of us. I hesitated before realizing I was ravenous. Deciding it looked normal, I peeled off the skin before tearing into the juicy fruit.

Mak managed to eat ten mangoes in the time it took me to finish mine. Luntian and Iska sidled over to the giant, making him laugh as they pestered him for mangoes of their own. I reconsidered my earlier thoughts about the kapre. *Perhaps he's not so scary after all.*

Bato stared at Iska like he still couldn't believe his bakunawa was being so friendly.

"Maybe Luntian is right," Kiri mused. "If Mak wanted to hurt us, he'd have done so by now, right? He might be a trickster, but he only wants to protect the creatures that live here. Maybe kapre aren't all as bad as the stories make them seem."

I frowned. "We can't escape in any case. There's no way we're climbing out of here ourselves—and even if we could, trying to navigate the forest at night is a death sentence. We're stuck with Mak whether we like it or not, and if he really does need us to get his belt back, we should be safe until then."

Still, Kiri's words made sense. Perhaps there was something the stories hadn't told us. About how not everyone who claimed to be a friend was trustworthy—and not all monsters were monsters at all.

"Get some rest," I told my companions. "I'll stay awake and keep watch."

At least, that was what I was *planning* to do, but I hadn't counted on how tired I was. The long hours of walking, getting lost, and all our terrifying experiences had combined into a heady mixture that was more potent than Datu Atay's coconut drug. It wasn't long before the soft crackle of the fire lulled all three of us to sleep.

☽

I was woken the next morning by a swooping sensation in the pit of my stomach. I cried out as huge fingers hoisted me into the air.

"Wake up, humanlings," came Mak's eager voice. "We go find Mak belt now."

Clutched in Mak's opposite fist, Kiri and Bato spluttered awake, their hair tousled and spiky.

How could you let yourself fall asleep? I thought frantically. *You were supposed to be keeping watch...*

I cast Kiri a helpless glance. This was our third rude awakening of the journey, and I was starting to believe that we'd never get a full night's rest.

Mak climbed agilely up the inside of the tree and leaped back down to the forest floor outside, causing a mini earthquake as he landed.

"We haven't even had breakfast yet," I groaned.

Kiri managed to wiggle his sash free. He tossed me a mango—a commendable feat considering that Mak's fists were swinging as he walked.

"Wow, thanks," I called back. The mango was a lot on the squished side, but it wasn't so bad once I tasted the sweet juice.

After a few minutes of walking up the mountain, Mak set us down. A rocky cave led into the ground, overgrown with trees and shrubs. It was impossible to see past the dark entrance.

That's what he calls "a little hole"? Still, I could see why the kapre couldn't go down there himself—the cave's entrance was too narrow for even his hand to fit inside.

Kiri looked puzzled. "If your belt is in there, then can't

you just rip this cave to smithereens?" he asked Mak. "I mean, you *are* the self-proclaimed Destroyer after all."

Mak gestured animatedly toward the foliage that grew all over the cave's craggy top. "Kapre *never* kill tree. Kapre only kill humans when they kill tree."

I gulped. "Okay, so we just go in the cave, grab the belt, and bring it back?"

Mak nodded.

Easy. Or at least I hoped it would be.

Still, I hesitated. Inside was pitch-dark, and I worried that we might fall onto sharp rocks or deep water. Or maybe there was nothing at all, and we'd just be falling, falling, falling . . .

"Iska," Bato commanded. "Light."

As sparks flickered around Iska's jaws, Mak gave a horrified shout and flung the bakunawa away from the cave. Iska flipped over and over in midair, dizzy.

"No fire in forest!" Mak yelled.

As Bato lunged toward the kapre in fury, I grabbed him by the sash and hurriedly asked, "Is there any other way we can get some light in here?"

Ignoring Bato's glower, the kapre calmly pulled out the long pipe from his waistband and puffed at the stem. A hovering blue light rose out of the bowl. The spirit circled my head before stopping near my shoulder. When I stepped forward, the light followed.

We all stared in astonishment until Mak coughed pointedly.

"Right," I said. "The belt."

I took a deep breath and eased into the entrance. I quickly found footholds and climbed down to the cavern floor.

"That was surprisingly easy," said Kiri as he and Bato landed behind me.

The hovering flame spirit illuminated the rocks and fissures of the cavern in an eerie, pale blue. I didn't see Mak's invisibility belt, but the cave was far bigger than what it seemed from the surface. Several dark tunnels led deeper inside.

I didn't know how long we spent searching in the flickering dark, going carefully to make sure we remembered the way back out. We squeezed through a narrow tunnel that opened into a round, smaller chamber. As the flame floated in, I was incredibly relieved to see Mak's belt—a length of woven fabric decorated with a thousand small circles of metal—lying on the ground.

Then my relief became all-out panic as I saw the sleeping creature curled around it.

"What *is* that?" Kiri yelped. Bato clamped his hand around Kiri's mouth when the creature snorted, rolling over.

The monster looked vaguely human, its skin mottled gray, two batlike wings protruding from its back. Its head resembled a wild dog's, and its fingers and toes ended in wicked claws. It was an aswang.

If I hadn't already slain a manananggal, seen a bird that could turn people to stone, and been carried in the hands of a living, breathing kapre, I think I would have fainted.

Kiri looked like he still might. I hoped that it would stay asleep—otherwise we might become some appetizing snacks.

The sensible part of my brain was telling me to run for it. The adventurous, competitive part of me hated not accomplishing what I set out to do. And the sister in me knew I would do anything to rescue Ligaya. I needed to somehow fish out the belt without the aswang waking up . . .

I crept slowly toward the sleeping creature, not daring to even breathe. Although I was terrified, the situation somehow reminded me of tiptoeing around the house with Ligaya, ready to go on a new adventure, knowing that even the slightest sound would wake my mother and get us into big trouble.

See? I told myself. *You've already done this a hundred times.*

Up close, the aswang smelled of burnt coal and rotten things. Illuminated by the blue flame, it looked even more frightening—its face was all crags and divots, the color of ash. Some people said that aswang transformed into beautiful humans to disguise themselves, but if that was so, it clearly wasn't true when they were sleeping.

If I was careful, I could reach past the aswang's tangled limbs and lift Mak's belt from the floor without disturbing it. But then the monster snuffled, shifting so that its skeletal arm rested on top of the belt like a baby curling around their favorite toy.

Great.

If I waited any longer, I would lose my nerve. I grabbed one end of the belt and slowly eased it out from under the aswang's arm.

The belt's metal discs scraped against the floor of the cave. The aswang's fingers twitched. I lifted it up, slowly, slowly . . .

Finally, the belt was in the air. I looped it around my body as best I could, cringing as the discs rang together. Hurriedly backing away from the still-snoring aswang, I gave Bato and Kiri a thumbs-up.

My companions were practically dancing on their feet. They were already halfway out of the chamber, beckoning to me furiously.

All too happy to join them, I quickly ducked into the side tunnel that led back to the main cavern.

Then I heard the growl.

My blood froze. I looked back to see the aswang's eyes snap open—they were yellow with horizontal pupils, like a goat's.

I stared in horror as it lunged toward me.

"Tani!" Kiri grabbed my arm and yanked me through the tunnel. A heartbeat later, the aswang slammed into the tunnel entrance, the span of its wings preventing it from coming through the narrow space. Needle teeth snapped shut just inches from my face, a wave of putrid breath washing over me.

"Hurry!" Kiri shrieked. By the glowing orb's light, we dashed through the twisting tunnels, not caring about scraping our shoulders as we heard the rasp of leathery wings squeezing through the narrow ways behind us. Once we were back in the main cavern, we desperately climbed toward the fading sunlight.

Bato made it to the surface first, reaching down to help Kiri, then me. Right before he hauled me to safety, I caught a flash of yellow eyes in the darkness just below my feet.

Mak was playing in the grass with Luntian and Iska. They looked so peaceful I wanted to shake them.

"An aswang's coming after us," I gasped.

Mak took one look at the terror on my face and was on his feet in the same instant. He sucked in a deep breath and gave an almighty puff on his pipe. Blue fire streamed from the bowl, right down the mouth of the cavern. Our hovering ball of flame danced away and merged with the magical fire.

Blinding light exploded from the cave. I staggered backward, shielding my eyes. Out of the cavern came a terrible shriek, like metal screeching against metal, as the aswang was incinerated. The ground shuddered as rock shattered somewhere far below.

I opened my eyes. Kiri, Luntian, and Iska looked dazed. Even Bato was shaken.

"Aswang gone," said Mak casually, as if he was informing me of the weather. He gazed at me expectantly.

Oh. Right.

I unslung the invisibility belt from my shoulders. Mak

wasted no time in taking back his belt and, true to his word, pulled out the Adarna's cage and handed it to me.

The bird looked indignant, but unhurt. As soon as I undid the latch, the Adarna burst out in an explosion of rainbow feathers, fluttering to the nearest tree to preen itself.

Kiri scrambled behind Mak, making sure that the giant was between him and the cave. "Please don't act like that was a normal occurrence," Kiri gasped.

I couldn't believe that Mak was taking this so lightly, but then again, the stories said kapre could live for hundreds of years. The idea that humans could die so easily—and that most of us didn't have magic blue fire to protect us—was probably completely new to him.

"No matter. Mak got belt. Humanling got pretty bird." He smiled. "Everyone happy."

"Ugh," Kiri groaned, which told me that he was feeling the exact opposite of happy. "After almost becoming that thing's dinner, I need to sleep for a month."

Mak nodded, squinting into the setting sun. "Humanlings rest in Mak home tonight. Then Mak let them go tomorrow." For a moment, he looked almost sorrowful. "Mak sorry for tricking you. Mak sad when you leave."

I sighed through my teeth. We'd spent almost a whole day searching for a belt when Ligaya was still missing. A part of me wanted to keep going, but after narrowly escaping the aswang, I knew we all needed the rest if we were going to save my sister.

Not a single day passed without my regretting falling for Mutya's wicked trick and giving up Ligaya as the price. No amount of honor or glory meant anything without her— and that was why it was up to me to bring her home.

Chapter 17

That night, we sat on the floor of Mak's balete tree, bellies full of fresh fruit. Mak sat by the blue fire, using a cloth to polish the metal discs on his belt until they reflected the light like tiny suns.

Suddenly, a vibration ran through the tree's roots and all the way up my body.

"It's probably just animals," Bato said, grabbing another rambutan from the pile on the floor.

Mak tied his belt around his waist and peered at Bato. "Not animals. Animals sleeping now."

Just then, a roar like thunder boomed through the night. The rambutan fell from Bato's fingers.

"Outside," Mak rumbled. *"Now."*

Without warning, the kapre scooped us up and bounded to the top of the tree. The earth was shaking even more, leaves shivering on their branches. We searched around wildly, trying to find the source of the quake.

The thunderous roar became almost unbearable.

"Look!" Kiri pointed up. "The moon!"

I craned my neck to look and almost fell out of Mak's fist.

The moon was disappearing.

The pearly orb had been almost full tonight, but before our eyes it shrank to half, then a quarter, of its size. Before long, only a thin crescent remained hanging in the sky.

Beneath the moon stretched a massive dark shape. Bony points protruded from its spine and huge jaws gaped wide. A serpentine shadow so great that it blocked out hundreds of stars.

Great Bakunawa.

I could scarcely believe it, but Babaylan Awit was right. The mighty Serpent herself, mother of all bakunawa, had emerged from her decades-long slumber and returned to swallow the last moon.

I'd dreamed of this moment since I was born: of when I would face Great Bakunawa and slay her once and for all. But right now, that hopeful vision couldn't be further from the truth. I wasn't a Serpent Rider. I wasn't a warrior.

Great Bakunawa was here, and I couldn't do anything to stop her.

Mak howled, shaking his invisibility belt so that the metal discs rang together like gongs.

Thrown up and down in the kapre's swinging fist, Kiri,

Bato, and I managed to wriggle our way free onto Mak's shoulders. We added our own voices to the cacophony.

"Go away, you beast!" Bato yelled, waving his sword. "Leave our moon alone!"

Far below, lights appeared on the shoreline as the inhabitants of Kalinawan—my people—ran out onto the beach. I imagined the villagers shouting at the top of their lungs, beating drums as hard as they could, desperately hoping that the noise would force Great Bakunawa to spit out the moon.

Loud noises had warded off Great Bakunawa before. With most of our Serpent Riders out looking for Ligaya— and me utterly helpless—the strategy had to be enough.

But only the thinnest sliver of the moon was left. One more swallow and it would disappear.

Please, Great Bakunawa, I begged silently. People and animals depended on the moon's light to survive. Without it, the world would never be the same.

Suddenly, a horn blast blared from somewhere in the forest, drowning out all of our shouts. I knew that sound— Swordmaster Pai's war horn. The horn blew again, and again, and again. The sound pulsed through my body, shaking my bones.

And then, finally, it worked.

With a last raging cry, Great Bakunawa spat out the moon.

Letting out a roar that shook the stars, the mighty

Serpent dived beneath the ocean in a spray of seawater, a fierce whirlpool appearing in her wake as she disappeared into the depths.

Moments later, the sea was calm. The moon shone steadily from the sky, perfectly whole.

Great Bakunawa was gone.

Chapter 18

Clinging to Mak's shoulder, I stared at the sea, unable to believe that a massive moon-eating serpent lay waiting in the murky deep.

The shocked faces of my companions proved that I wasn't imagining things. After all these years, Great Bakunawa was back. And I knew she wouldn't be warded off so easily next time.

A loud flapping sound, like a flock of birds taking flight, pulled me from my thoughts. High screeches pierced through the forest.

My face went cold. Our shouts had scared off one kind of monster, but as it turned out, they'd also attracted another.

Aswang.

We all exchanged horrified glances. "Hide, Mak," I whispered urgently. *"Now!"*

Before the giant could move, the first of our attackers burst through the trees.

The aswang in the cave was scary enough, but in the moonlight, this aswang's grayish skin stretched back from its gaunt monkey's face like a death's head. Long, spindly arms tapered to wicked claws.

The stink of sulfur rolled out from each beat of its wings as the monkey aswang arrowed toward us. Four more animal-headed aswang burst through the leaves, each more terrifying than the last.

"Swords!" Bato yelled as Iska reared, sparks spitting in the back of her throat.

Iska's fire blast turned two aswang into burning cinders. Luntian managed to drench another in water, but it only made the creature twice as angry.

"Ice!" Kiri shouted at his bakunawa. "Turn it to ice!"

Luntian flicked his fins, but nothing happened. Pivoting on Mak's shoulder, I slammed my sword into the aswang's body, sending it plummeting to the ground with a furious shriek.

Before we could seal the victory, five more aswang soared toward us.

"There are too many of them!" Bato shouted as a pair of the monsters came within range of his swords. He managed to fend one off, but would have been impaled on a second creature's claws if Mak hadn't crushed the aswang in his giant fist. Thrown off-balance, we clung to Mak's hair to keep from falling.

The kapre scrunched his eyes as he concentrated hard.

My skin shivered strangely. I looked down to see that my entire body was transparent as glass.

We're invisible, I thought in amazement. I could barely see the outlines of Bato and Kiri beside me.

The aswang stopped mid-flight, whirling in confusion as they wondered where we'd gone. Mak leaped off the branch. My stomach lurched as we free-fell before landing with an earthshaking *boom*.

I wanted to scream, but I knew that any noise would tell the creatures exactly where we were.

"Mak," I hissed. "Quickly, use your blue fire! They won't stand a chance if you—"

"No," Mak interrupted, sounding defeated. "Mak can't use fire."

Before I could ask why, Kiri spoke up. "If Mak unleashes his blue fire at the aswang, then he'll burn his own home down as well." He looked at me. "We have to lure them out into the open. Bring them all together, then incinerate them."

I nodded, but we didn't have much time before the aswang discovered us. Thinking fast, I pointed to a spot nearby. "Over there!"

Mak ran in that direction.

"Now, stop being invisible," I said.

In a blink, our bodies returned to their natural colors. Dozens of malicious eyes swiveled toward us.

I gulped. "Now run!"

Mak pounded through the foliage, trees shaking with

each powerful stride. The aswang were quick to chase, zipping through the air like oversized bats. I held on desperately to Mak's shoulder.

I blanched to see that the aswang were only moments away from catching us. "Invisible!" I yelled.

Once more, we flickered out of sight. The aswang stopped, spinning confusedly, giving Mak a few precious moments to catch his breath. But his loud gasping quickly caught their attention and they shot toward us with renewed vigor.

Crashing wildly through the forest, we alternated between being visible and invisible to keep the aswang on our trail. When some got too close and snapped at Mak's face, he plucked them from the sky and flung them against the ground, where they landed with loud *cracks*. But there were far too many of them for Mak to take out by brute force alone.

Finally, we burst into a wide, treeless clearing.

This is as good a place as any.

Right on our heels, a horde of aswang poured out of the forest like the gates of the Lower World had been flung open. They flew across the moon like a living, breathing storm cloud. Just how many of them *were* there?

"Mak," I shouted. "Fire! Now!"

The kapre pulled out his pipe, took a huge breath that seemed to suck all the air from the sky, and blew on the stem with all his strength. A blue inferno roared out of the opposite end, blazing into the night.

The blast was so hot it felt like all my skin was about to melt off. I scrambled for shelter behind Mak's hair.

Shrieking aswang dropped out of the sky like falling leaves, burning to ash the moment they touched the flames. I turned away, trying not to be sick at the acrid smell of scorching flesh.

But then—impossibly—still more came.

The blue inferno became a stream, then a flicker, as Mak ran out of breath.

"Feel . . . dizzy . . . ," he moaned.

"Behind you!" Kiri shrieked.

The kapre spun, raising his pipe to his lips once more. But he had barely summoned his breath when the new horde of aswang set upon us. One monster snatched the pipe out of Mak's hands, cackling. Mak did his best to swat away as many as he could as we clung to the kapre's hair for dear life.

"Why aswang attack us?" Mak shouted, flinging off a creature that raked sharp claws down his face. The kapre was desperately trying to activate his belt's magic, but it was impossible to concentrate.

To my shock, one of the creatures answered. This one had the head of a tusked boar, and was far bigger than the rest—clearly their leader.

"My name is Razok," replied the aswang, his face eerily calm in the moonlight. His voice was a strange mix between a human timbre and a boar's growl. "We are sent by the

Mahika. These human children do not know the danger of the path they walk—and so, they must be stopped."

With a howl of triumph, all the aswang swooped down as one. Mak fell to his knees beneath the creatures' weight.

Screaming, I swung my sword into the nearest monster. It crumpled around my blade, but it was replaced by another, and another, and another.

On Mak's opposite shoulder, Bato gave a panicked yell as a pack of aswang swarmed him all at once.

Kiri yelped as an aswang caught sight of him tangled in Mak's hair. Tearing my eyes away from Bato's quickly disappearing form, I grabbed a lock of Mak's hair and climbed down the kapre's back.

Unslinging my sash from my shoulder, I swung it as hard as I could at the aswang attacking Kiri. The heavy bakunawa egg tied inside conked the monster right on its temple. It fell away in a crooked spiral.

"We have to get out of here!" Kiri's voice was almost drowned out by the ragged flapping of aswang wings. Beside him, Luntian whimpered.

"How?" I shouted back.

But Mak had heard us. Using one hand to swipe away as many aswang as he could, he combed his other hand through his hair until he held all three of us in his fist. "Humanlings escape. Now."

"But what about you?" I cried. "You can't possibly take on all these monsters by yourself."

Mak gave me a strange look. "It all right," he rumbled. "Save the princess."

The words confused me before Ligaya's face swam into my mind. The kapre couldn't possibly be talking about anyone else.

"My sister?" I demanded. "What do you mean?"

"Adarna tell Mak about beautiful princess," Mak said. "Mak know now that she is special."

The kapre pulled back his arm, and it was too late when I realized what he was doing. "No, no, no—"

Mak flung his arm forward and his fingers disappeared.

I was airborne.

Chapter 19

I hurtled through the night like a comet. More like a broken doll, since I flipped over and over so many times, I thought I was going to be sick.

Sky and land blurred before my eyes. Two specks of color flashed by as Kiri and Bato floundered beside me, screaming.

But we weren't the only ones in the air. A trio of dark shapes hurtled toward Bato, their wings tucked tight. While I struggled to orient myself, the aswang snatched my helpless friend in their talons and flapped away.

"*No!*" I yelled.

Roaring in fury, Iska streaked after her master. The Adarna wheeled wildly in the air as it struggled to evade another aswang chasing its tail. Moments later, they all vanished from my sight.

My stomach heaved as the cold wind scraped my cheeks

raw and brought more tears to my eyes. Then something suddenly shifted in my sash. My bakunawa egg hurtled out of the cloth as the last of the knots came loose.

Frantically, I tried to grab hold of it, but the wind snatched the egg from my grasping fingers. It glimmered faintly as it plummeted to the forest far below.

Even this high up in the air, an ice-cold weight settled in my chest.

I just lost my bakunawa.

I thought that my situation couldn't possibly get any worse.

I began to slow down. For a fraction of a second, I hung suspended in midair, thousands of trees spread out beneath me.

Then I began to fall.

"Ahhhhhhhhh!" I wildly pinwheeled my arms as if I would suddenly grow wings and fly. I reached toward the distant sky, begging one of the stars to catch me.

"Oof!" I slammed into the forest canopy. "Ow!" A branch was kind enough to break my fall. "Ouch!" Leaves whipped into my body as I ricocheted from tree to tree.

And then there was only the ground rushing toward me at a dizzying speed. I squeezed my eyes shut and waited for the inevitable *crunch* . . .

A hand grabbed my ankle, slowing me down just in time.

"Tani, I got you!" Kiri shouted. I craned my neck to see Kiri holding on to my foot. And wrapped around *his* legs was a frazzled Luntian, struggling to keep afloat with the extra weight. Despite the bakunawa's best efforts, we slowly dropped lower and lower . . .

I spat out mouthfuls of dead leaves as my face dragged along the ground. Then Kiri lost his grip and all three of us collapsed in a heap.

Kiri smiled weakly at Luntian. "Thanks."

Luntian gave an exhausted growl.

Once we caught our breath, Kiri asked quietly, "Do you think Bato will be okay? How are we going to find him?"

Annoying as Bato's over-the-top bravado was, his unshakable confidence was what had kept us going this long—even if I'd only ever wanted to prove him wrong. It was impossible not to notice his and Iska's glaring absence, and even now, I half expected him to pop out of the foliage, laugh at me for being such a hopeless leader, and remind us once again that he had everything under control. Terror, exhaustion, and despair chased each other around my head. I couldn't imagine how Bato was feeling, alone and probably badly injured, if not worse.

"I'm sorry," I said, hating how weak I sounded. "I don't know what to do."

I was afraid to offer up another plan, because all of mine seemed to only worsen our situations. A heavy silence passed.

Kiri fished something out of his sash. "If it helps, I have these."

Two metal discs lay on his open palm.

"Are those from Mak's belt?" I asked.

Kiri nodded. "They came loose during the battle with the aswang. I was going to give them back, but I never got the chance after . . ." He mimed tossing the discs like Mak had thrown us.

"Perhaps they can turn *us* invisible too," I said excitedly as Kiri handed one to me.

Then I frowned. Even if the discs' magic worked on us, I didn't know what use invisibility would be when we were lost. Being invisible wouldn't protect us from hunger, the cold . . . or the aswang.

I was shaken to my core. I couldn't believe they were following the Mahika. I always believed the Mahika was a beacon of hope and light, but there was no doubting the magician's wickedness. First, Mutya abandoned her people, then she took my sister captive, and now she commanded an army of aswang. If the stories were wrong about her, what else were they wrong about?

Perhaps the stories were wrong about you, *Tani. They said that you would be your father's daughter, that you would save the moon—but you can't even save your sister, or your friends.*

I let out a shaky breath, clenching my fists in my lap.
Don't. Think.

"We'll figure something out," Kiri said after a long moment. Then he added in a small voice, "Hopefully."

Above us, the constellations glimmered through the canopy. I could see the Warrior's Star that Kiri, Bato, and I had all been born under. Across the sky lay the Story Chanter's Star, Ligaya's constellation, which destined her to a life of seclusion as the beloved princess.

Now Ligaya was missing and Great Bakunawa was here. My people believed the stars told us our fates, but right now, I didn't feel like a brave warrior who would rise to protect our moon. I felt like a little girl—lost and lonely and afraid.

Kiri leaned back against a tall earthen mound. For the first time, I noticed that it was one of many mounds in this part of the forest. They almost looked like they were built here on purpose.

We lay there, lost in our own dark thoughts, as the stars gleamed above us in the night.

☽

Sharp, spindly things poked into my arms and back.

I gasped awake, ready for fight or flight—then bit back a scream as I came face-to-face with a giant black ant.

The insect was *seriously* big. The ants back home were no bigger than grains of rice, but this one was about the size of a small dog.

This is a dream. Wake up. But the sun was shining high above the trees, meaning it was morning. And I could feel all the scrapes and bruises from my crash landing in the forest.

I watched with horrified curiosity as the ant clicked its mandibles. More huge ants scurried out of the dirt mounds I'd noticed the night before, a whole army of them winding toward us. The ground trembled beneath my feet—was it from the force of their march, or was it just me shaking in fear?

"Are you seeing what I'm seeing?" Kiri whispered, rubbing his eyes. "Please say you're not."

"We're on Mount Mahiwaga," I hissed back. "Nothing should surprise us anymore."

I slowly drew my sword. Last night, we landed right in the ants' territory, though we'd been too disoriented to notice. Now I hoped we wouldn't have to pay for that mistake.

The ants shuffled menacingly closer, dozens of sharp stingers glinting in the light.

Kiri flinched back. "Something's watching us, Tani. Something *else*. In the trees."

Peering through the foliage, I saw small beady eyes staring back through the leaves—eyes that looked *almost* human . . .

Then the earth shuddered again, stronger than before, making us stagger. When I looked back, the eyes had disappeared, but whatever caused the sudden shake didn't stop the insects' advance.

"We can't fight them all off!" In a flash of inspiration, I remembered what Kiri had given me the night before. "If we use Mak's invisibility discs, we might—"

"Too late!" Kiri swung his dagger as the nearest ant raised its stinger toward him. Before either sharp object could connect to its target, the ground lurched and threw us both off our feet.

Kiri's dagger missed the ant by a mile. But it didn't

matter, because all the ants went tumbling through the air as the world began to shake like something alive.

I landed hard on my shoulder, pain spiking through me. After I finally managed to stand, I tried to help Kiri up, but I could barely keep my own balance on the heaving ground.

"It's an earthquake!" Kiri struggled to his feet. As the forest shuddered and swayed, the ants became a roiling black sea in their haste to escape, completely forgetting they had wanted to sting us just moments before.

My mind was still reeling. This land was no stranger to earthquakes—small ones that were barely noticeable most days. Why had this one happened so suddenly? And there hadn't been one *this* strong since . . .

Since Great Bakunawa last devoured one of the moons. Last night, the Moon Eater and harbinger of disaster had emerged from her exile—and all her devastating powers had returned with her.

Trees shivered around us, ancient branches splintering above our heads. The ants weren't a threat anymore, but if we didn't get to a clearing soon, we were as good as finished.

"Run!" I barely avoided being crushed by a falling branch as we fled. Kiri pulled ahead of me, dodging ants that scrambled all over the place in their frenzy to escape. I could tell from his panicked movements that he had no idea where he was going.

A weird sound made me stop short. It was a high-pitched

whistle, like wind rushing through a gully. It was coming from right below me.

I leaped over a fallen log, following Kiri, when I saw what was making the noise. A tiny old man with a long, wispy beard lay pinned beneath the log, his frantic eyes finding mine. Instead of words, the high whistling sound screeched from his mouth.

Was it you who was watching us before? Cracks fractured the ground as the twisting tunnels beneath the ant-hills gave way. I was running out of time—and if this old man was responsible for the ants earlier, then it wasn't worth saving him.

But the small creature kept screaming. Though I couldn't understand him, his meaning was clear: *Help!*

I desperately wanted to save myself. But I couldn't bring myself to abandon the small man—he wore the same expression of terror and despair Ligaya had when she was kidnapped by Mutya. I hadn't saved Ligaya then, but this old man still had a chance. And I knew that if I left him here, he would die.

With a strength I didn't know I had, I set my shoulder to the log and pushed with all my might. Slowly, the huge log rolled off the old man's leg. His face twisted in pain and relief.

Suddenly, his eyes widened as he pointed right behind me.

I turned just in time to see a giant tree, shaken from its

roots, teetering in place. Then it began to fall, bearing down toward us with inevitable force.

I instinctively dropped to the ground, dragging the old man with me into the shelter of the log that had trapped him. The tree crashed down with a resounding *boom* right above our heads. Its impact jolted through me as it split the log in two.

The loose earth below our feet gave way. Dirt showered me as we fell into the anthill, plunging us into darkness.

And then the world fell still.

It happened so quickly that the sudden silence rang in my ears. By the light filtering through a crack in the earth above us, I saw that the old man beside me looked shaken but unharmed. We'd fallen into one of the anthill's chambers—and the massive tree that almost crushed us was blocking our exit. And I knew there was no way I could lift *that*.

To my surprise, the old man smiled. He reached for something in the pocket of his tunic—a wooden flute. Lifting it to his lips, he played a lilting tune.

Moments later, I heard dozens of scurrying legs, then something lifted the tree, clearing a path.

The ants, I thought. *Why are they helping us?*

We crawled back onto the surface, spitting mud. The entire forest was a splintered ruin, the roots of felled trees reaching out from the dirt like skeletal fingers. I shuddered to think of what could've happened if I hadn't been lucky enough to survive. I took a long moment to catch my breath.

Sure enough, the ants were back—though instead of

looking threatening, they regarded me with curiosity. And standing among them were more tiny old men, as tall as my hip with long white hair and beards, staring at me like they'd never seen a human before.

One of the old men, leaning on a wooden staff, rushed forward and embraced the one beside me. They began speaking in voices that sounded like flowing water. With a start, I realized that this was their language.

The one with the staff turned to me. "Thank you," he said hesitantly. Even speaking the human language, his voice was musical, spun from nature. "Thank you for saving Apong, our leader. He tells me that if you hadn't freed him, he never would have reached the Wood Flute in time to call our ants for help."

Apong, the flute player, beamed at me. That was *one* good sign—if the flute was the secret to commanding the ants, then maybe Apong wouldn't command them to attack me again after I'd rescued him.

The old man beside Apong bowed apologetically. "My name is Karyo. Like Apong and my friends, I am a nuno, one of the keepers of the anthills. Humankind doesn't often venture to this mountain, and they have done great harm to the engkanto, so we sent our ants to frighten you out of fear for our own safety. Now I see that we were wrong. Perhaps not all humans are as evil as we thought."

One of the ants affectionately bumped its head against my leg. I patted it awkwardly, relieved that I'd made the right choice after all.

Apong whispered something to Karyo. "Our leader is asking how the nuno can possibly repay you for saving him," Karyo translated. "Though I struggle to think of a gift that would equal Apong's life."

The answer came easily. "My sister," I said immediately. "She was kidnapped by the Mahika and taken through this forest. Have you seen her?"

Karyo thought for a moment before shaking his head. "We haven't seen another human girl pass through here. But as soon as we rebuild our home, I promise to send our ants to find her."

I nodded and thanked them for their help, but I had to get moving. Besides Ligaya, somebody *else* was missing. I had no idea where Kiri had gone after we got separated. And after what just happened, I didn't trust my friend to stay out of trouble if I didn't find him soon.

Chapter 20

Kiri!"

After the first hour of screaming his name, my throat felt rough as sand. Still, I didn't give up.

"Kiri!"

My shout disappeared into the ruined forest, swallowed by the silence.

The longer I searched, the more scared I became. I *wanted* to believe Kiri was all right, but I knew that he would never leave me behind on purpose. He could have been injured in the earthquake or gotten lost in its aftermath. Or maybe he was in far worse danger . . .

Sunset bled across the sky, then night fell. I was hopelessly lost with no friends and no bakunawa. There was no way I'd find my egg in these twisting trees—not that it would have been much use anyway. Now that it was dark, *anything* could be watching me, and I wasn't liking my chances of surviving alone.

As the darkness deepened, glimmering flames appeared through the gloom, arranging themselves into a path through the forest. The fire spirits could lead me to safety . . . or, more likely, to my death.

"I'm not following you," I said.

The fire spirits flickered. I ignored them until they shifted to form a ring, hovering above something nestled in the leaf litter.

I strained to see through the darkness.

Then an iron fist clenched around my heart.

"No," I whispered. "No."

The fire spirits scattered as I rushed toward them. Strewn among the rocks and leaves lay several shards of something speckled with glittering colors.

My egg! But how could that be? It was impossible to break a bakunawa egg until the creature itself was ready to hatch. After falling from the sky, it looked like my egg had shattered.

Dust fell from the broken segments as I gathered them into my hands. Between the pieces, I saw tiny pale shapes glinting in the moon's weak light.

They were bones. Bakunawa bones.

I didn't want to look, but the truth was there.

My bakunawa is dead.

Broken memories flashed through my mind. One moment I was training with Swordmaster Pai, and the next I saw Bato telling me that I didn't deserve to be a Serpent Rider. Then came the sleepless nights I'd spent sitting in front of this egg, hoping with all my being that my baku-nawa would hatch.

Now it never would, because my bakunawa was noth-ing but dust. *Has it been dead all this time?*

I remembered what Ligaya said before, how she'd sensed something wrong about my egg.

Heartbroken, I realized she was right.

All I ever wanted was a companion—to have a unique bond like that of a bakunawa and their rider. Someone who would fight alongside me no matter how uncertain the odds. I'd been waiting my whole life for my dear friend, only to find out I was waiting for nothing at all.

How could this have happened? Only those born beneath the Warrior's Star could bond with a bakunawa. And I *was* a warrior. Just like Bato and Kiri, I *had* been born under the Warrior's Star . . . hadn't I? My entire life was built on the hope that I would one day defend our last moon against Great Bakunawa. To become a legendary hero like my father.

Or maybe, whispered a dark voice in my head, *the Spir-its didn't think you were worthy of being a warrior. Haven't you always known you aren't strong enough to defeat Great Bakunawa? You can't protect* anyone, *Tani.*

Losing Uling was painful, but this was infinitely worse. I wasn't just holding a dead bakunawa—I was holding the shattered hopes of the world, of our moon, in my hands. *I* was supposed to be the one who would protect the moon, and without a serpent of my own, that destiny was lost forever. I didn't deserve to wield the blade of my father, the greatest rider who had ever lived. How did I ever believe I could live up to him?

The fire spirits watched me as I cradled the remnants of my egg, the pieces just as broken as I was.

Chapter 21

Slowly, fearfully, I tucked the fragments of shell and bone into my sash. I couldn't bring myself to leave them lying on the forest floor.

How was I supposed to protect our moon if I wasn't even a real warrior? How was I supposed to rescue Ligaya?

Suddenly, a frantic cry tore through the trees. My heart leaped into my throat.

It wasn't Ligaya. But I recognized that voice.

Kiri.

I sprang to my feet, drawing my sword, as my warrior instincts kicked in.

Serpent Rider or not, I still had a friend to save.

I ran toward the shout. My feet snagged on vines and roots, but I angrily cut them away.

Now I could hear the shout clearer. *"Help!"*

Soon I smelled smoke and cinders, sulfur and rot. The hair on the back of my neck stood on end.

Aswang.

I shivered and gripped my sword tighter. I hoped I could get to Kiri in time.

Holding my breath, I shuffled forward as the leaf litter on the forest floor muffled my footsteps. Before long, the ground in front of me dropped away into a deep abyss—a massive gorge banked by sheer cliffs on both sides.

I crawled forward on my belly and peered over the edge, heart thudding behind my ribs.

It was swarming with aswang.

They clung to every free space on the rock, some hanging upside down like bats, others crouching and polishing their claws. All of them were chanting in hissing, guttural voices.

At the foot of the cliff, an animal-headed creature held a slumped Kiri in its claws. For a moment, I feared the worst, but then I realized my friend was frozen with fear. Luntian struggled in the grip of another aswang, who held the bakunawa's jaws tightly shut.

I wanted to yell out a battle cry and charge in to save my friend, but another, more sensible part of me knew that trying to take on all those aswang by myself would only put Kiri and Luntian in more danger.

The aswang holding Kiri flapped toward a fissure in the ground that bubbled with steaming hot water. It was a natural hot spring, but I had the sinking feeling it was about to become the aswang's giant stew pot.

A boar-headed aswang glided down into the gorge. I recognized him as the leader who had spoken to us in the fight at Mak's balete tree.

"Mmm," Razok hissed between his curving tusks. "We haven't had human for dinner in a long, long time."

Another aswang stirred the bubbling water with a long branch, like a cook mixing soup. He even threw a few roots and leaves in for flavoring, smacking his twisted lips in relish.

The monsters began to sing in jagged, unearthly voices.

Stir the water now and then,
spill the blood of tasty men.
Tremble at the terror seen,
when Mutya will become their queen.

Kiri's face turned as white as chalk. He struggled and kicked at his captor's claws, but remained helplessly stuck. My hand clenched around my sword. I was badly outnumbered, but I had to do *something*.

Just before I was about to leap down the rocks, Razok's head snapped up. His boar snout twitched, sniffing the air.

"Mortal," he hissed. "I smell another mortal."

Then I heard wings flapping toward me as the smell of sulfur blew into my face.

I scrambled back into the meager shelter of the trees, burrowing beneath leaves and fallen branches. As the aswang shot out of the gorge, I held my breath, hoping they wouldn't see me. But too late, I remembered I'd forgotten to sheathe my sword.

The aswang screeched in triumph as they caught sight of my gleaming blade. Their faces stretched in wicked grins as they surrounded me.

Giving up on my hiding spot, I surged to my feet and swung my weapon in a deadly arc. The aswang flinched away, but they soon swooped toward me, their claws sinking into my shoulders. I cried out as they dragged me toward the lip of the gorge. I tried to punch, kick, dig my heels into the ground, but my fate was certain.

"Two mortal children." Razok screeched gleefully from below. "We will feast tonight!"

"Tani?" Kiri's shocked gaze snapped to mine. "Get out of here!"

Before I could shout back that I wasn't going to just leave him, the aswang's chanting grew louder and louder. I choked on the creatures' rotten stench. Then the ground disappeared, and my kicking feet dangled over open air.

"No!" I shouted.

The aswang let go.

I plummeted, arms wheeling desperately. A cackling aswang caught me at the last moment. I sucked in a breath as I flipped upside down, the monster grasping me by my ankles.

"Mortals are so scared of flying," it growled in my ear. "You should learn to grow some wings."

I hung above the boiling pool of water as other aswang brought Kiri and Luntian closer. Fighting to see through the hissing steam, I saw my own terror reflected in Kiri's eyes.

"What is it you humans are so fond of saying?" the aswang behind me asked. "Ladies first."

The aswang began to lower me toward the steaming liquid. The end of my sash sank into its depths, the mixture frothing around the cloth and eating it away.

I didn't even want to think about what it would do to my skin.

From down on the ground, Kiri screamed my name.

Wait . . . on the ground?

I craned my neck to see that the aswang who had been holding Kiri was flapping around in bewilderment, staring at its empty claws. Kiri himself was nowhere to be seen.

A moment later, my friend appeared out of thin air, standing on the rocky floor. He looked terrified but unhurt. He must have used one of Mak's discs to escape the clutches of his captor.

"Tani!" he shouted again, waving his arms. In his hand was the jar of medicine that Babaylan Awit had given him.

In a flash, I understood.

As I struggled to free my own jar of ointment from my sash, Babaylan Awit's voice echoed in my head. *It's deadly to monsters; that is why it is so effective . . .*

My hair submerged in the water, dark strands sizzling.

Kiri opened his jar and threw it into the spring. The steam quickly grew acrid with the smell of bitter medicine.

"Hurry, Tani!" Kiri yelled.

Sweat poured down my face in sheets. My fingers slipping on the lid, I finally opened the jar and flung it down into the roiling water.

With steam billowing past my face, I almost didn't notice the aswang who was holding me suddenly droop. It coughed violently, struggling to stay aloft as its death grip on my ankles loosened.

With the last of my strength, I swung upward and grabbed the aswang's shoulders, kicking my legs free of its claws and pushing off its body to swing away from the hot spring. I landed on solid ground, only inches away from falling in.

The unconscious aswang tumbled headfirst into the boiling spring, sinking beneath the bubbles without a sound.

Shuddering, I saw aswang dropping from the sky like dead bats as they inhaled the medicinal steam, hitting the ground with leathery *thumps*.

Kiri fell back in surprise as an aswang almost landed on him. Just then, a yelping Luntian crashed down on Kiri's stomach, knocking the breath from his body.

I ran over. "You okay?"

"Not really, to be honest," came the weak reply as I helped him to his feet. "But at least we're alive."

We stood together among the bodies of fallen monsters. Two warriors, victorious on the battlefield. Despite having been only heartbeats away from becoming aswang stew, I couldn't suppress the grin that stretched across my face.

"We did it, Kiri." I shook my head. "I mean, *you* did it. Thinking of using Mak's invisibility disc and Babaylan Awit's medicine was just . . . wow."

Kiri flushed. "Thanks," he said, smiling. "I'm really glad we're both okay."

"Seriously, that was the bravest thing I've ever seen. Courage isn't just about charging into battle and swinging a sword. There are other ways to be strong too—like standing your ground when you could have just as easily run away. Thinking quickly is just as important as acting quickly."

Before Kiri could respond, a pile of rocks behind him suddenly rattled. To my horror, Razok and three dog-faced companions exploded out from behind the boulders.

Kiri and I quickly backed away. I shifted my grip on my kampilan, but I didn't know what a puny metal weapon could do against creatures who had defeated a mighty giant like Mak.

Razok's black gaze roved over the slumped forms of the other aswang before fixing on us. His fathomless stare bored into my skin like a sharp blade.

But instead of the powerful wingbeats I'd come to expect from the aswang, I noticed the monsters flew crookedly. They hadn't escaped the deadly steam as well as they'd hoped—it was like someone had conked them over the head.

Still, they could possibly shake off the medicine's effects. And to make matters worse, the foliage on either side of the gorge began rustling, as if something was moving through the forest beyond. That only meant one thing: more aswang were incoming.

I had to act *now.*

"Look! Tani, it's—" Sounding surprised, Kiri grabbed my arm. I shook off his grip and charged straight at Razok.

Despite his apparent frailty, Razok quickly lashed out with a sharp claw and caught me across the ribs. Gritting my teeth, I swung my sword in a lethal arc that ended in Razok's arm.

Iron bit into flesh. The aswang gave a howl of agony as his severed hand spun away into the dark.

I shifted my feet, breathing hard. Razok's tusked face loomed above me, the stump of his arm oozing dark blood. If the aswang were angry before, now they were beyond furious.

And then I felt the steam from the hot spring waft against my skin. If I took a single step in the wrong direction, I'd tumble into the boiling water.

I was cornered.

Though my heart was hammering, my fists clenched tighter around my sword. Swordmaster Pai's voice filtered back to me: *Whatever you do, do not show fear.*

"Let us go," I said, and was surprised by the power in my own voice. "Or I'll slice off your other hand too."

Even with a severed arm, Razok laughed. His twin tusks gleamed dully between cracked lips. "Are you so arrogant, mortal, to believe that you can command an engkanto?"

Before I could answer, all four aswang dived down as one.

Suddenly, a stream of fire shot out from behind me, searing heat blasting past my face. An aswang howled in agony before dropping to the ground, trailing smoke. And then—to my utter shock—I heard a bakunawa's roar.

Chapter 22

I whirled around, hardly daring to hope. Had Bato managed to fight off the aswang who carried him away? Had he found us?

But the person behind me wasn't Bato. Instead, he was one of the older Serpent Riders, fighting alongside his fire bakunawa as the serpent held the aswang at bay with its ferocious breath.

Thick arms wrapped around me and lifted me into the air. I felt a jolt of surprise before I glanced up into the stern face of Swordmaster Pai, his serpent-scale armor glinting in the light.

My cheeks coloring, I struggled in his grasp. *I'm not a little child!*

"You fought well, Tanikala," Swordmaster Pai said firmly, "but this is not your fight."

After realizing I couldn't break free, I stopped struggling as my teacher carried me to safety.

More Serpent Riders and their bakunawa rushed past us to join the fight. Jets of water and shards of earth whistled through the air. The triumphant expression slipped from Razok's face as he saw that he was outnumbered.

Swordmaster Pai set me down away from the battle.

"How did you even find us?" I asked breathlessly.

"You can thank yourselves for that," he replied. "After you three disappeared from Kalinawan, everyone was frantic trying to figure out where you went. Imagine our surprise when Babaylan Kalan-ya looked into her magical fire and saw the three of you standing over a manananggal's smoking ashes." Despite his stern expression, his eyes glowed with pride. "You were gone by the time we got there, but then a rainbow bird—the Adarna—found us and led us straight to you. And it seems we arrived not a moment too soon."

Kiri was practically dancing with delight. "Swordmaster Pai! You came! We're saved!"

I should have felt relieved, but all I could feel was intense sadness.

Though I'd been only a hair's breadth away from being eaten by aswang, seeing the bakunawa reminded me of my own egg. I could still remember it lying in pieces on the ground.

By the time I looked back at the fight, three aswang lay motionless on the forest floor. Razok flapped away into the sky, one of his wings bent at a twisted angle. No matter how many powerful bursts of elemental magic were shot toward him, the aswang had flown too far out of reach to be hit. Before long, he vanished over the lip of the gorge.

I clenched my fists. *We let him get away.*

Swordmaster Pai looked at Kiri, then at me. "Where's Bato?"

When I didn't reply, my teacher's face darkened with worry. But before I could tell him what happened, two familiar figures pushed through the warriors.

Though her face was worn from travel, Datu Eeya didn't look any less imposing as she and Babaylan Kalan-ya marched toward me.

The sight of my mother was more terrifying than all the aswang combined.

The last time I'd seen her, she'd forbidden me from leaving my room . . . yet here I was, halfway up an enchanted mountain.

But my mother didn't look angry. Instead, I saw an uncharacteristic furrow between her brows.

"Tanikala," she said with a quaver in her voice.

With a start, I realized my mother wasn't about to scold me. The strange expression on her face was worry. I felt a brief flash of guilt—I could count on my fingers the times I remembered her being *worried* about me. Then my hand drifted instinctively to my sash, which no longer held the familiar weight of my bakunawa egg.

I pulled out the egg's shards. Swordmaster Pai and the other Serpent Riders gasped at the sight of the shattered shell. Kiri looked as though someone had struck him across the face.

My mother was the only one who kept her composure. To my shock, she wasn't perturbed in the least—instead, her lips pressed into a thin line. Babaylan Kalan-ya placed a gnarled hand on her shoulder.

I stared at them blankly. "Why are you looking at me like that?"

The two women remained silent, looking at the remnants of my egg. Cold dread crept up my spine. "Were you *expecting* this to happen?"

A faint flush of color rose in my mother's cheeks. Babaylan Kalan-ya shifted uneasily.

Is nobody going to explain this to me? As my confusion grew, a spark of fury kindled in my chest. What were they hiding?

And then Datu Eeya spoke. "You know the story of your father, don't you?"

Of course I knew the story. Everyone in Kalinawan did. My father had been a hero, but how was that related to my bakunawa egg?

I glared at my mother. A hint of sadness entered her gaze.

"You, Tanikala, were born on the day that he died," she said simply, having relived this sorrow many times over.

"I already know that," I said angrily. What was she trying to do—make me pity her? "I was born at midnight on the day my father was killed, under the Warrior's Star."

"Except you weren't," said Babaylan Kalan-ya in a voice as dry as coconut husks. "There were many stars in the sky on the night you were born, Tanikala, but the one that watched over your cradle was not the Warrior."

What? My hand seized tight around my father's sword—my instinct when I was nervous or afraid. With an effort, I forced myself to let go. I noticed that the rest of the Serpent Riders—including Swordmaster Pai—looked just as stunned by this revelation as I was.

Had my mother and the babaylan kept this secret for all these years?

The words rushed out of me. "But you told me I would have a bakunawa. You told me I would save our moon— that I would be a Serpent Rider."

Instead, my hopes and dreams had been broken as easily as my egg had been.

Datu Eeya stared at the ground. "Your father was Kalinawan's greatest hero. We all thought *he* would save the last moon. After he died, we were devastated. We needed something to believe in—we needed a new hero, someone to give us hope that we could stand against the Moon Eater when she returned. Without hope, I feared the Serpent Riders would completely lose the will to fight. Then our moon would truly be lost."

"So you lied to us all that *I* would carry on my father's legacy." I frowned. "But because I wasn't born beneath the Warrior's Star, my bakunawa was never going to hatch. It died instead."

"Do not blame Babaylan Kalan-ya," my mother said quietly. "After you were born, she begged the Spirits every day to grant you a bakunawa, but I told the lie to everyone. By the time I thought better of it, the damage was done—everyone believed that you would be the one who saved the moon."

So this was how it had always been. Even now, I couldn't escape my dead father's shadow.

The babaylan's face was solemn. "Do not despise your mother, Tanikala. She thought she was doing what was best for us all."

I tried to imagine my mother twelve years ago—her husband killed on the same day her first daughter was born. She'd been young, confused, and terrified, and hiding the truth from the villagers was the only thing she could think of.

But it didn't mean it was *right*. Is that why she'd always been so cold and distant to me and Ligaya? Was it because she'd chained one of her daughters to a legacy she could never live up to, no matter how hard she tried?

Babaylan Kalan-ya wasn't finished. "Despite everything, Tanikala, your birth gave us the hope we desperately needed. The Serpent Riders trained harder than ever, believing *you* were the hero reborn—and though you do not have a serpent of your own, we have dozens ready to fight Great Bakunawa, more than we've ever had before. And the time to prove themselves has come."

I turned away, fuming. I couldn't remember a single day

I hadn't dreamed of the time my bakunawa would hatch and I could be a real warrior. Datu Eeya hadn't meant to tell an outright lie, but she had kept the truth of my birth from me nonetheless. I couldn't believe I'd been betrayed by—of all people—my own mother.

And even though Babaylan Kalan-ya wasn't solely responsible, she was in the wrong too. For so long, I had thought of the old woman as family . . .

Datu Eeya looked at the ground. "I'm sorry, Tanikala."

Her tone told me that she really meant it, but at that moment I wanted to shake her. Those scant words were hardly enough to make up for it all. Perhaps they never would be—and both of us knew that.

As my hands clenched into fists, Swordmaster Pai gripped my arm. "Calm down, Tani."

I still wanted to hit something, but my teacher's cool voice and my battle training forced me to focus on my breathing as I struggled to control my emotions.

Swordmaster Pai went on. "We all saw Great Bakunawa rise from the ocean and try to swallow the last moon. The Great Serpent returning at the same time the princess was kidnapped can't be a coincidence. And we heard what the aswang were singing. They serve the Mahika, and she's the one keeping Ligaya captive."

In the grim faces of the warriors around me, I sensed the sting of Mutya's betrayal—that the one who was gifted supernatural powers to protect the world had now turned against us. The flames of my anger cooled as my teacher's words sank in. Whatever I'd discovered about my past didn't change the fact that my sister was still in danger.

Swordmaster Pai placed his hands on my shoulders, forcing me to meet his gaze. "I've always told you that it is the choice we make in a span of a moment, when there's no time left to think, that tells us who we really are. So, Tanikala, the choice is yours. What will you fight for?"

I looked back at my mother. Her face was set once more into its usual expression of calm and poise, but her eyes were shining, begging me to forgive her.

A part of me didn't know how I could ever accept her apology. *But she's not the only one who has made mistakes.*

Even now, the guilt of losing Ligaya gnawed at my gut like poison. Although I would never have wished it in a thousand years, it was still my fault that Ligaya was gone.

The truth was that *all* of us felt anger, fear, and sadness. Sometimes those emotions were enough to push us over the edge. Perhaps, despite how much we tried not to, we all did things that we would come to regret.

I looked at Swordmaster Pai. Even without a bakunawa, he was the most formidable warrior I knew. He didn't need a magical serpent to prove his worth on the battlefield.

More than that, I realized my teacher was right. No matter how I felt about the secrets my mother and Babaylan Kalan-ya had kept from me, or my own guilt that I had tried to cheat my way to being a Serpent Rider—those things were already in the past and couldn't be changed. Now we all had to put aside our grievances and work together for a goal that was far more important: fix our mistakes as best we could.

And that meant only one thing.

We had a princess to save.

Chapter 23

As we clambered out of the gorge, I spotted a bright flash of color in the moonlight. The Adarna perched on a nearby branch, its feathers twitching impatiently as it watched us.

My heart thudded with hope. The Adarna would lead us to my sister. That meant Ligaya still had a chance.

Wasting no time, the rainbow bird clacked its beak before gliding through the trees.

"Onward!" said Datu Eeya, holding her dagger high. "For Princess Ligaya. For Kalinawan. For our moon."

The urgency in her tone jolted everyone into action. We surged through the forest, chasing the Adarna.

We made a formidable force—around two dozen warriors gripped iron weapons as their bakunawa's powerful magic prepared to ignite. Even my mother held a dagger in each hand.

The sound of wheezing made me stop. Babaylan Kalan-ya struggled up the trail, leaning heavily on her staff.

"Are you all right?" I asked.

"I take the eggs from right under Great Bakunawa's nose," she gasped out with a grin. "I can handle a stroll through the forest, can't I?"

And then, as if the mighty creature had been summoned by the sound of her name, a thunderous roar shook the sky.

Even the brawniest, most battle-scarred Serpent Riders flinched at the sound. Nobody spoke, but I could see the fear in their eyes.

Great Bakunawa is here.

The last time she emerged from the sea to swallow the moon, we hadn't been prepared. But now, we would be ready.

We had to be.

The echoes of the roar faded away, replaced by the sound of crashing waves as the air grew sharp with the smell of salt. The full moon beamed brightly in the sky. Would this be the last time we ever saw it?

Fear lanced through me as another thought crossed my mind. If Great Bakunawa was here, what did that mean for Ligaya?

We picked up the pace to a near-sprint, following the Adarna as it sped through the forest. It flew almost faster than we could keep up, as if it wanted us to hurry—as if we were running out of time.

We broke through the foliage and emerged onto a ridge that overlooked a spur of rock jutting out over the sea.

I braced my hands on my knees, trying to catch my breath before I had a proper look at the sight before me.

Beyond the mountain stretched the endless sea, the water a stormy, brooding gray.

And then my stomach shriveled. Standing on the ledge right below us was Ligaya, her dress tattered, long dark hair whipping around her face in tangled locks. At her shoulder was Mutya who stood gazing at the ocean. Crashing spray burst over the edge of the cape, showering my sister in water. Her hands were bound by a heavy metal chain embedded deep into the rock, preventing her escape.

Throughout our arduous journey, the thought of being reunited with my sister was what had kept me going. I hadn't expected flowers and sunshine when I found her—she was a captive after all—but even still, seeing her now felt like a punch to the gut. I never foresaw *this*.

"If the princess you will find, break the chains that bind," Babaylan Kalan-ya said softly, repeating her prophecy. Her words confused me before. Now their meaning was painfully clear.

What was Mutya doing to my sister?

And then it hit me—the cold, horrible truth, moments before another mighty roar shivered through the ocean depths.

I remembered what Ligaya told me on the night we sat together at the forest's edge, looking at our world's last moon.

The only way to stop the Serpent from devouring the moon

is to give her a sacrifice that can stand in the moon's place.
A sacrifice just as pure, just as beautiful . . .

All the blood in my veins turned to ice.

Mutya was going to sacrifice my sister to Great Bakunawa.

Chapter 24

I couldn't believe that the only things separating me from Ligaya were a few spurs of rock. But with Mutya standing right beside her, I didn't know what to do.

Then an eerie scratching sound filtered up toward us. Sharp claws and leathery wings appeared on the sides of the rock as swarms of aswang climbed the craggy face to surround Mutya and Ligaya.

"Come to me, my loyal servants," Mutya said as the aswang approached, their animal eyes shining with loyalty and devotion.

The Mahika's voice softened, becoming almost tender. "You, Razok, and your kin have always been my friends, even when all the others abandoned me."

Razok came to the front of the pack, his wing still bent at an odd angle. "We follow only you, our Mahika," he rasped.

"That's because your heart is evil," Ligaya spat at Mutya

with a glare. "The stories say that the Mahika must use her powers to care for all living beings. But because you let your heart become wicked and rotten, the good creatures of this mountain fled from you, and that's why only the foulest monsters want to serve you."

The venom in my usually kindhearted sister's voice took me aback. Mutya hissed and I instinctively grabbed my sword, wondering if Mutya was going to strike her. But then Mutya's hands fell back to her sides—the Mahika no doubt thinking Ligaya's watery fate was punishment enough.

Mutya's face contorted in anger. "You don't understand, *little girl*. Nobody understands. I only want to protect our world . . . and this is the only way."

My sister looked dubious, but perhaps the malevolent looks from the aswang kept her silent. Then Ligaya gasped as the heavy chain creaked, its iron links magically tightening around her hands.

A huge shape moved beneath the water, and I caught the glint of thousands upon thousands of silver scales, gliding through the current as easily as a sword cut through air.

Mutya rubbed her thin hands together as her gaze flickered across the waves. I knew she was waiting for the perfect time.

Great Bakunawa was almost here.

Despite my fear, my hand closed around the hilt of my kampilan. I'd already failed Ligaya once. Now I'd rescue her from the jaws of the Moon Eater if it was the last thing I did.

Before I could take a single step, Kiri's icy fingers dug into my skin. "Even *you* can't fight that many of them, Tani."

As usual, he was right. I thought the aswang in the gorge had been enough monsters for a lifetime. But here, there were *hundreds* of them. I hated to admit it, but this many foes would prove a challenge even for the bravest Serpent Riders.

My blood boiled, but my anger was tempered by the helplessness that threatened to drown me. Everyone else looked just as hopeless as I did.

How could we possibly fight against all those aswang?

Suddenly, something brushed my knee. At first, I thought it was just the dense foliage behind me, but then the tap came again, more insistent.

I turned and saw an old, wizened face framed by a wispy beard. The being stood no higher than my hip, still repeatedly tapping my knee.

I was so stunned that it took me a few moments to recover my voice. "Apong?"

The nuno gave a broad grin. He spoke rapidly in words that sounded like birds chirping.

"Apong says he is very happy to see you again." Beside Apong, Karyo appeared from behind a low shrub, bowing respectfully.

"Who are these beings?" Datu Eeya asked warily.

"We are the nuno of the anthills," Karyo said proudly. He turned to me. "We have marched across the whole mountain in search of you, to pay you back what we owe."

Datu Eeya watched our exchange in confusion. "Tanikala, what in the world are they talking about?"

"No time to explain," I said hurriedly. "Karyo, Apong, you have to get out of here. It's not safe."

Before I even finished speaking, the grumbles and growls of the aswang below abruptly fell quiet. Razok's head snapped up, sniffing the air.

"What is it?" Mutya's sharp voice drifted up to us.

"Mortals," Razok hissed, his face twisting around his protruding tusks.

Mutya's brows drew down. "You didn't kill them both like I told you? They're only two children!"

Razok shifted uncomfortably. "It wasn't just the two young ones, my Mahika. The warriors from the seaside village—and their serpent companions—came to rescue them at the last moment." The aswang shuddered. "They slaughtered many of us."

Mutya clenched her fists, showing no regret at this news. She appeared to have forgotten about my sister for the moment, but I could see Ligaya straining against the too-tight chains.

Karyo spoke up. "Are those creatures of filth hunting you?" The burning hate in his eyes surprised me.

I nodded emphatically. "They very much want to see us dead."

Apong and Karyo exchanged glances. Slowly, they stood up straight, their faces set in determination.

Apong said something in the voice of crackling fire.

"You saved our leader's life," Karyo translated. "Now it is our turn to save yours."

"What?" I gasped. "Can't you see how many monsters are down there?"

Apong smiled. He patted his belt, and I saw the Wood Flute tucked into the strap. I looked at it thoughtfully. Maybe, with the flute's power on our side, we would stand a chance.

Several aswang prowled toward the ridge where we were hiding, coming to investigate what Razok had smelled.

The battle was almost here.

Noticing my troubled expression, Karyo patted my arm reassuringly. "Do not worry. Apong and I have not come alone."

Apong raised the Wood Flute and played a soft melody. The foliage behind us rustled. The Serpent Riders instinctively grabbed their weapons.

A wrinkled face peeked through the leaves—then two, then three. More and more nuno appeared out of the undergrowth, accompanied by a troop of huge black ants, until about fifty of the dwarfish beings were crowded on the ridge.

As one, they looked to me, their eyes shining with purpose.

Karyo bowed with a hand to his heart. "Our lives are yours."

Chapter 25

U p there!" Razok suddenly cried, pointing a hooked finger toward our hiding place. Without meaning to, my eyes locked with his.

A triumphant smile curled his lips. "Found you."

And then, by some unspoken command, every single aswang surged up toward us.

Swordmaster Pai's war golok hissed through the air as he brought it aloft. "For Ligaya. For Kalinawan!"

With a wordless cry of fury, the Serpent Riders rushed down the ridge to meet our attackers. Above, the full moon illuminated the rock in almost blinding radiance. The aswang looked even more terrifying in the harsh white light.

The air exploded around me as the bakunawa opened fire. Aswang howled as they were incinerated by flame, thrown by the wind, or pierced by shards of ice and earth.

"Luntian!" Kiri yelled. The emerald-scaled serpent spat a powerful jet of water that caught an aswang full in the face.

It crashed into one of its fellows and the two went down in a sodden heap.

"Good, Kiri," Swordmaster Pai grunted. He swung his sword into the crumpled creatures, sending them flying off the cape and into the sea.

The sound of clashing weapons rang out as our forces collided. Serpent Riders swirled and danced, attacking the aswang with blade and fist. Their bakunawa were equally deadly with their sharp horns and powerful jaws.

I slashed out with my kampilan as an aswang flew straight toward me. The tempered iron slammed into its head, knocking the aswang to the ground. I didn't even have the chance to make sure it was down for good before another aswang swooped in to replace it. Before long, my breath rasped through my chest and my muscles ached with strain.

Right behind us, the nuno clung to the backs of their ants like a cavalry of small riders. They carried coils of vine rope, twirling them over their heads before flinging them at the hovering aswang. The ropes were tied into loops that drew tight over the aswang's bodies, trapping them fast. Working in teams, the nuno fought to bring the monsters down.

As I flung myself away from a cat-aswang's raking claws, Apong pulled out the Wood Flute and began to play. His fingers flickered deftly over the instrument, notes and trills blending into an intricate tune. The melody grew to a crescendo.

The earth trembled beneath my feet. When I looked back at the forested ridge, my mouth dropped open.

A horde of wild animals burst from the trees and raced down the slope. Goats, pigs, monkeys, and even water buffalo stampeded into the fray, churning up a cloud of dust in their frenzy. Bird calls filled the air as a flock took to the sky, diving down into the swarm of aswang.

The aswang cried out in fury as the animals attacked with hooves, teeth, and talons. A rampaging water buffalo crashed into a horde of aswang, skewering two on its horns, while a trio of boars attacked a third monster with their vicious tusks.

I gazed at the Wood Flute in awe. Of course—if the instrument's magic could command the ants, then it could very well command all the beasts on the mountain too.

The Adarna joined the fight alongside its kin, raking the aswang with its sharp beak. But even with all these new allies, there were still far too many enemies.

To make matters worse, jagged streaks of lightning plunged down from the sky, meeting the sea in explosions of blinding light. Thunder built behind the clouds as Great Bakunawa's powerful magic stirred up a storm.

And then, amid the chaos of battle, I heard a voice call my name.

"Tani!" Through the press of fighters, Ligaya stood alone beside Mutya, her gaze finding mine. Mutya grabbed Ligaya's arm, holding her fast.

White-hot fury rose in my chest, threatening to explode.

You will not take her again.

Snarling, I batted aside an injured aswang and ran to my sister as fast as I could.

Vast leathery wings obscured Ligaya from my sight as a dark shape rushed into me. Pain lanced across my body. Too late, I pressed a hand to my chest where Razok's sharp claws had slashed three lines into my skin.

The boar-faced aswang looped back before diving down into another attack. Razok was far bigger than his comrades, and it took all my strength to parry his blow.

Even with a damaged wing, Razok was terrifyingly deadly. His lips peeled back in a mirthless smile. "I let you escape me twice, young mortal. There will be no third chance."

My chest burned like fire each time I took a breath. I could hear the sea below me, the crash of waves slamming against rock—but I couldn't fend him off for much longer.

Then I took a step back and felt my heel come down on nothing but air.

My stomach swooped as I teetered on the edge of the precipice. At the last moment, I reached out for something, *anything*, to grab onto. My hand clamped tight on the severed stump of Razok's wrist.

Razok looked amused. He raised his other hand, its claws wicked in the moonlight. "I never got the chance to thank you for this," he said, nodding toward his stump. "Now I get to return the favor!"

As his curved claws descended upon my arm, I let go with a gasp.

And then I was falling.

The sea grew louder and louder as I plunged toward the depths. Razok hovered above me, a triumphant smile on his lips.

Suddenly, bright copper scales flashed across the moon as a stream of fire blazed toward Razok. Caught off guard, the aswang beat his wings powerfully and barely evaded the blast.

Iska circled back around with a roar. The bakunawa snapped her jaws, tearing off a ragged chunk of Razok's wing. Howling in agony, Razok spiraled away and vanished from my sight.

Wasting no time, Iska dived after me like a copper arrow. But I could already feel the salt spray freezing my skin. In a few heartbeats, I would be underwater—and, far below the waves, I could sense something watching me.

"Tani!" Seated on Iska's back, holding on for grim life, was Bato.

Even though I was grateful to see him again, I would never have predicted what he would do next. Without hesitation, Bato leaped off Iska's back, stretching a hand toward me.

I grabbed his arm instinctively. Just when I was sure we would both slam into the jagged rocks below, Iska wrapped her coils tight around Bato's legs. My body jolted as my fall was cut short. We hung suspended over the sea, mere inches from certain death.

Hanging upside down, Bato reached down his other hand and grasped my arm, flinging me up and over onto Iska's back. I held on to the copper serpent's horn as Bato swung up behind me. Iska flew us back to the top of the cape where the fierce battle still raged.

Safely back on solid ground, I collapsed with exhaustion. Footsteps approached and I looked up to see Bato standing over me. Even now, I couldn't believe that he was here. After losing him in the forest, I didn't think I'd ever see him again. But for some reason, he looked different . . .

I gasped. A crooked red scar traced its way down his face, narrowly missing his eye.

Bato noticed my expression. "You know what I said before, about being able to take on thirty monsters single-handedly?" He thought for a moment. "Make that . . . twenty-five."

I stared at him. I couldn't believe he was in a mood to joke about this. A thousand questions wanted to burst out of me, but they were all summed up by just one. "How are you even *here*?"

"Well, right before Iska incinerated the aswang that were coming after me, I made one of them tell me where Princess Ligaya was being taken." Bato shrugged. "I just followed its directions."

"But you *survived*!" I spluttered. "The aswang, the forest . . . everything!"

Bato patted Iska's scales affectionately. "I had help. Couldn't have fought off all those monsters without Iska—or survived falling out of the sky. And . . ." He hesitated. "I used some of the tricks you used on me, when we sparred before. Well, not some. A *lot*."

I was still so stunned that I didn't even think to feel gratified—even though that was the closest thing to praise I'd probably ever get from him.

"Besides, you and Kiri already had *one* epic fight without me. I'm not going to miss out on another one." He offered me a hand.

I glanced at his outstretched palm. Then I gripped his wrist and Bato hauled me to my feet. We looked at each other.

Suddenly, a stray fireball from the battle whizzed in our direction. Bato ducked away before his eyebrows were singed off.

"Let's go!" With that, he ran back into the battle.

Chapter 26

The sight before me was absolute chaos. Blades flashed, bakunawa growled, and animals screeched as our ragtag army attacked the aswang relentlessly. My spirit sang to see that there weren't nearly as many enemies as there were before.

Swordmaster Pai snarled as he fought atop a hill of aswang that he'd felled with his fearsome war golok. Dozens more of the creatures lay crumpled on the ground, not even moving when drops of cold rain began to fall from the sky.

The one who looked most in shock was Mutya. The Mahika stared in disbelief at her vanquished forces, holding poor Ligaya's wrist so tightly that I was terrified she'd snap my sister's arm.

I snatched my father's sword from the ground and started running. But I wasn't the first to reach them.

"Release her," my mother demanded, leveling her daggers at Mutya. "You've already lost."

Mutya glared. "You forget whom you speak to, *mortal.*"

The wandering woman let go of Ligaya, who gasped in relief. Then she began moving her fingers like she was plucking the strings of an instrument.

The Serpent Riders cried out. I glanced around wildly, wondering what was happening, before I saw Swordmaster Pai bring his sword around to hold off an aswang. He moved too slowly, then his arms stopped moving altogether. The aswang barreled into him and the two went down in a heap.

Mutya's dark gaze found mine. Suddenly, I couldn't move my feet anymore. It was like they were stuck fast, unable to leave the ground. Stuck to . . .

"My shadow," I whispered. "She's holding our shadows!"

The aswang spied their chance and prepared for a final, mighty charge.

If they attacked us now, we were finished.

Dark magic crept along my skin, slowly claiming control of my limbs. Soon I would no longer be able to move my hands.

If only there was a way to cut off my shadow!

And then the solution came to me, as bright as the moonlight.

If I'm invisible, I won't have a shadow.

Almost at the end of my strength, I reached into my sash and grasped Mak's invisibility disc before Mutya's spell could stop me completely. I felt my skin shiver as my whole body became transparent as the air.

Sprinting forward, I tackled Mutya. As we fell to the ground, the invisibility disc flew out of my grip, crumbling to dust as I became visible again—but I had done all that I needed to. As long as I kept Mutya from casting her shadow spell, the Serpent Riders could fight back.

A cry pealed through the night as the Adarna took to the sky. Mutya hissed, struggling in my grip, but I held her fast because my life depended on it. The rainbow bird opened its beak and sang.

The Mahika's eyes widened as her fingers turned a sickly gray. Moments later, her hands had turned to stone, preventing her from casting her evil spell. The stone crept up her forearms . . . her elbows . . .

The Adarna screeched in panic as a shape collided with it midair. Razok, his injured wing dragging, sent the Adarna flying into a spur of rock with a powerful punch. The magnificent bird squawked as it crashed into the rock, slid down its surface, then lay still.

Ligaya screamed.

The rain was falling harder now, making the clustered fighters look like wraiths moving through the mist. Fire bakunawa hissed unhappily as their flames sizzled out, but the water bakunawa came alive with renewed energy.

As Razok swooped down to finish the Adarna off, Luntian, hovering beside Kiri, flicked his tail. A glittering point of ice scythed through the air and hit Razok in the chest.

The lead aswang tumbled end over end with the force

of the impact. An expression of sheer incredulity appeared on his face before his strength gave out at last and he toppled into the sea.

Kiri, Bato, and I ran to the edge of the cape. I saw silver scales moving in the depths, the glint of needle-teeth opening wide, then Razok disappeared in the blink of an eye. Nothing but a trail of bubbles marked his passing.

Shivering, I turned back. Mutya was on her knees, staring at her petrified hands.

"Give up, Mutya." Babaylan Kalan-ya stepped forward. "It's over."

A hint of recognition flickered across the Mahika's face. "It must happen like this," Mutya wheezed. "To sacrifice a young soul to Great Bakunawa, as pure and beautiful as the moon. We've already lost six of them. Nothing else will work—this is the only way to sate the Serpent's hunger."

Babaylan Kalan-ya's face clouded. Now that the two women were side by side, I was struck by how similar they looked—while the babaylan was older and Mutya looked young, they were surely related to each other somehow.

"After I drove the Moon Eater away, I spent many long years traveling the lands, seeking the perfect offering." Mutya looked straight at Ligaya. "Finally, I have found the one."

"Please, Mutya," begged the babaylan. "Release the girl. We can find another way. There is always another way."

Mutya flinched as if the words inflicted more pain than

any of her injuries from the battle. As the rain poured down and lightning forked along the sky, she smiled.

"It's too late, my dear sister. Great Bakunawa is already here."

At that moment, her voice was swallowed by a tremendous roar, louder than ever before.

Chapter 27

We all fell to our knees as the ground shuddered beneath our feet. Swordmaster Pai was the first to recover, his face whiter than the fog.

"It's coming down!"

The rock itself was crumbling away beneath us. I heard a smashing, grinding noise as something massive grated against the cape.

Kiri grabbed my and Bato's hands and we sprinted toward the forest. My heart pounded more from terror than exhaustion—one wrong step on a loose rock could send me tumbling to my doom. I was dimly aware of Babaylan Kalan-ya helping Mutya to her feet as they desperately fled to safety.

If we can make it to the ridge . . .

To my relief, almost all the Serpent Riders, nuno, and animals had made it to the shelter of the forest, and we weren't far behind them.

But then I stopped short. In our terror-filled rush, some-one had been forgotten.

Ligaya screamed as the rock shuddered, barely able to hold the shape it had maintained for centuries. Huge waves crashed against the cape, drenching my sister from head to toe.

Though the blood turned to ice in my veins, I shook off Kiri's hand.

"Tani?" Bato yelled. "What are you doing? We have to *run!*"

Just then, a massive pointed horn rose against the hori-zon. It was covered with algae and clinging shells, and its tip was razor-sharp.

Ligaya strained against her bonds, but the chain was fas-tened deep in the stone and wouldn't budge.

Then a huge eye appeared beneath the horn. Its surface was opalescent, the pupil a dark vertical slit. Our terrified faces were reflected in its iris like a mirror.

As Great Bakunawa's eye swiveled onto her, Ligaya's legs gave way. The Serpent reared out of the waves, sheets of water pouring off her silver scales. Translucent fins, each one as big as the sail of a boat, rippled in the air.

With a roar, the mighty she-serpent revealed rows of jag-ged teeth—longer and sharper than any sword—set in powerful jaws.

Jaws big enough to devour a moon.

And then the rocky cape collapsed. Ligaya screamed as she plunged down . . .

Straight into Great Bakunawa's waiting throat.

Do something! a voice inside me screamed. But it was as if all my nerves were set alight, leaving me to feel both everything and nothing at once. All I could see was Ligaya falling into the Great Serpent's gaping mouth, a fractured moment that replayed over and over in my head.

Someone—my mother—wailed.

That sound snapped me back to reality. Swordmaster Pai ran through the rain with a pale-faced nuno under each arm. His eyes met mine, wide with fear and grief.

I remembered what he told me, at a time that now seemed so long ago. *It is the choice we make in a span of a moment, when there's no time left to think, that tells us who we really are.*

In that moment, I made my choice.

I ran to the edge of the cliff and leaped after my sister.

Chapter 28

My arms wheeled frantically as loose rocks tumbled away beneath my feet. Dimly, I was aware of people shouting my name, but it was all drowned out as Great Bakunawa's hot, putrid breath washed over me.

Below me, the Serpent's jaws gaped wide: a deep, bottomless abyss ringed by deadly teeth.

I only just avoided being skewered on a spiky tooth as I twisted in midair. A moment later, Great Bakunawa's jaws slammed shut, shattering the iron chain that held Ligaya captive. The world plunged into darkness.

"Oof!" The breath huffed out of me as I landed on something warm, wet, and soft. I shuddered in disgust as Great Bakunawa plunged into a dive.

An instant later, my body was flung back upward to slam into the roof of the Serpent's mouth. Somewhere in the sticky darkness, someone yelped.

"Ligaya!" I stretched out a hand in the vague direction

of the shout. Small fingers brushed mine before clamping tight.

Finally, we leveled out and Ligaya and I plopped back down onto the tongue. All my insides felt tangled in knots. Being absolutely covered in serpent slobber didn't help.

My stomach heaved, but I threw my arms around my sister. Ligaya returned the embrace, and though she was shivering, I sensed her relief that she wasn't alone in the dark.

"I'm sorry," was what I wanted to say, but the words choked up in my throat. Instead, I hugged Ligaya tighter, unable to believe we were together again.

After a while, I noticed that the world outside had gone eerily quiet. Fragments of sound pulsed and echoed strangely. We were underwater.

But that was a small problem compared to our current predicament. I'd be hard-pressed to think of a more dangerous place than inside the mouth of a moon-eating sea serpent.

I shuddered at the thought of those massive jaws clamping shut, with Ligaya and me trapped beneath rows upon rows of deadly teeth . . .

My sword came free of its sheath with a *hiss*.

"Don't even think about it!" Ligaya snapped.

I glared at her, more surprised than hurt. It dawned on me that my sister was no longer the soft-spoken girl who wove patterns in her room. She had changed.

Ligaya went on. "What do you think is going to happen

if you attack Great Bakunawa now? We'll get spat out at the bottom of the ocean!"

I lowered my sword with a sigh. She was right. Mentally, I kicked myself for forgetting one of Swordmaster Pai's most important rules: *Always use your brain before your fists!* But it was hard to think clearly when I was more scared than I'd ever been in my life.

For the first time, I noticed that Ligaya's hands were clasped together. She opened her fingers and a minuscule point of light floated out. A firefly.

"I met her in the forest," Ligaya explained. "I call her Ning."

I had to smile. "Ning? That's a pretty name."

Ning's presence, although small, comforted me. It was like we were in a vast cavern, one made of living flesh rather than stone.

"You look absolutely terrible," Ligaya told me. She looked just as frightened as I did, but I was grateful for her efforts to lighten the mood.

I shot her a mock scowl. "*You* don't look any better. Imagine what Mother would say if she saw you right now."

In a terrible imitation of Datu Eeya's voice, we chimed together, "*Young lady, wash your hair at once! You smell so bad that all the pigs will swarm to you for breakfast!*"

We both burst out laughing.

After a while, Ligaya grew uneasy. "It *is* getting rather uncomfortable, sitting on this warm, wet tongue . . ."

No sooner had she spoken than my stomach suddenly

heaved. We were pressed down into the bakunawa's tongue, sinking into its damp softness.

"What—" Ligaya gasped.

I flicked a string of spit from my eyes. "She's swimming *up!*"

I heard waves crashing as Great Bakunawa breached the surface of the ocean. Streams of seawater poured into the gaps between the Serpent's teeth, soaking us even more than we already were.

A solid impact juddered through my body.

Land.

Great Bakunawa opened her jaws and flicked her tongue, sending Ligaya and me sprawling onto a stretch of white sand. We staggered to our feet, beaten, bruised, and covered from head to toe in bakunawa drool, but I'd take any of those options over being devoured. Even the ferocious storm had abated, leaving the sky calm and clear.

I grabbed my sword and spun back to face the Great Serpent. But instead of snapping us up, the creature regarded us slantwise through one bright, intelligent eye.

"You're not going to eat us?" I was so incredulous that the question burst out of me.

Great Bakunawa rumbled deep in her throat. I was surprised to find that while her voice was much louder, she sounded exactly the same as Iska or Luntian.

Further down the beach, Ligaya gasped. "Tani! Look!"

She stood at the edge of a wide rock pool with clear water lapping at the sides. Looking at the pool, I realized how thirsty I was after the battle. Without stopping to think, I fell to my knees and gulped great mouthfuls of the cool, fresh water.

Suddenly, the strangest sensation ran across my body. I looked down to see the angry red slashes across my chest close over, until I couldn't tell they'd been there to begin with. All my other scrapes and bruises faded back into healthy skin.

Ligaya stared at me in wonder, then she too drank and was healed of her injuries.

It's enchanted water.

I pulled out my drinking container and filled it to the brim with the healing water. I had never seen this place before, but the sight of the rock pool stirred up a memory.

"Of course," Ligaya whispered. "The sacred pool of life-giving water, where Great Bakunawa lays her eggs."

Now I remembered the stories. Babaylan Kalan-ya told us that Great Bakunawa—though ever-watchful for a chance to escape her enchanted exile and devour the moons—needed to sleep for a single night every year, a sleep so deep that the tides were forced back with each mighty breath the Serpent took. That was when Babaylan Kalan-ya made her annual journey to collect Great Bakunawa's eggs from a special pool, the only place in the world that the eggs were laid. For fear that others would try to take advantage of the eggs and the water's medicinal properties, no one except the village babaylan could know its location.

Until today.

But why had Great Bakunawa taken us here?

Sure enough, round eggs in different patterns and colors lay in clusters at the bottom of the pool. Water hyacinths drifted on the gentle current, lending their own soft beauty. My heart ached at seeing the eggs, so peaceful and perfect, after what happened to mine.

"It's wonderful," Ligaya breathed. Then she tilted her head, spotting something over my shoulder.

With Ning zipping along beside her, my sister ran to a small cave on the edge of the beach. The inside was shadowed, untouched by the light of the moon.

"Be careful, Ligaya," I warned, keeping an eye on Great Bakunawa.

By the time I made it to the cave, Ligaya was standing inside, her mouth open in shock as Ning's faint glow illuminated the space.

I let out a quiet gasp.

Dozens of broken eggshells lay strewn upon the sand. Even shattered, the rainbow of color they reflected was breathtaking.

I knelt beside a familiar shell, picking up three brittle pieces that were pearly white, speckled with sparkling emerald.

"This is Luntian's shell," I whispered. But what was it doing here?

A strange, aching feeling grew in my chest. I spied more eggshells that glittered with the colors of fire.

Iska.

I turned and saw Great Bakunawa waiting in the sea, her magnificent form framed by the cavern's mouth. But this time, I wasn't scared.

"The eggs," I said slowly. "After they hatched and the shells were thrown into the sea, you brought them back here."

Great Bakunawa rumbled again, the sound lost and forlorn.

Still carrying Luntian's shell, I walked back across the sand to the rock pool. I imagined this was the same path Babaylan Kalan-ya took when she came here every year, collecting just enough eggs for the new children born beneath the Warrior's Star, and making sure the rest were destroyed.

Reaching the edge of the pool, I held the pieces of the egg together to imagine what it might have looked like sitting in the water, alongside all its brothers and sisters.

I pulled the shards apart. Between the fragments, caught upon the water's clear surface, the reflection of the moon rippled back at me.

The last piece of the puzzle fell into place.

"That's why you devoured the moons," I whispered. "Because they reminded you of your eggs. For all these centuries, you only wanted to be with your children."

Great Bakunawa swam a slow circle. Gently, I laid the pieces of Luntian's shell on the shoreline, which the mother Serpent tenderly nosed back into the cave. Ligaya returned a moment later, her face ashen.

For so many years, I was fixated on becoming a Serpent Rider to slay Great Bakunawa and protect the last moon.

I wondered what would've been different if I'd known what that really meant—if we had tried to understand Great Bakunawa instead of fighting her.

Even though the Serpent's eye was as tall as me, looking into it, I got the feeling she was staring straight through me. "Why did you bring us here?" I asked.

Ligaya surprised me with an answer. "Because she believes that we can fix this."

Fix this? My sister couldn't be serious. She might as well have suggested we try to return the six lost moons to the sky.

Everyone was raised to see Great Bakunawa as a terrible monster who caused typhoons and earthquakes, a monster who had to be stopped at all costs—and most of all, as the monster who had swallowed our moons. I couldn't even begin to guess how long it would take for an entire people to change that view.

But after what we had just seen, I knew we had to try.

Chapter 29

Swordmaster Pai was right. Riding on a bakunawa was the most exhilarating feeling in the world—especially when I was riding on the greatest bakunawa that had ever lived.

I let out a whoop as Great Bakunawa sped through the waves as easily as a blade cut paper, a current of whitewater streaming in our wake. We passed pods of wild dolphins who leaped high before diving deep beneath the waves. Seabirds swooped down from above, skimming the surface of the ocean with glittering fish trapped in their talons.

Here, I felt truly alive.

The sun had just begun to rise in the eastern sky. Ligaya and I clung tightly to Great Bakunawa's horn, my sister looking just as happy as I did. I almost didn't notice Ning the firefly hanging on desperately to a strand of Ligaya's hair.

Perhaps I was enjoying myself more than I thought, or maybe Great Bakunawa was just that fast, but it seemed only moments before the rocky headland where we'd fought our final battle emerged out of the morning mist.

Serpent Riders appeared on the edge, pointing and shouting as Great Bakunawa approached.

With horror, I realized they were planning to attack.

Thinking fast, I unsheathed my sword and held it up so the light of the dawn slanted off its iron blade. Swordmaster Pai gasped as he caught sight of my sister and me perched atop the Great Serpent's head.

Bato's mouth fell open as he appeared at Swordmaster Pai's shoulder. I waved at him with a grin.

As Great Bakunawa drew level with the headland, Ligaya and I jumped onto the ruined rock.

The Serpent Riders looked exhausted, but to my relief, I saw that most of the aswang lay dead or dying. Thanks to their skill and bravery, along with the help of the nuno and their animal friends, the battle had been won.

But there was still one enemy left to vanquish.

Several weary Serpent Riders stood around Mutya, who was kneeling on the ground as everyone discussed who would deal the datu's justice.

"I'll do it." My mother stepped forward, drawing her daggers. "She kidnapped my daughter after all."

"No." Ligaya's voice rang out, surprising us all. "This is my fight."

Swordmaster Pai looked stricken. "But, Princess—"

Ligaya cut him off with a glare. "I can take care of myself, you know. I've been doing it for the past few days."

My sister pushed through the circle of warriors until she stood over Mutya. I'd never seen my little sister look so angry.

Without warning, the wind picked up, sending Ligaya's dark hair dancing around her face. My sister clenched her fists and the wind gusted stronger.

"How are you doing that?" Mutya demanded, her face growing pale. "Only the Mahika . . ."

". . . can wield the powers of nature. I already know that—it's literally my job to memorize the stories." Ligaya's gaze hardened. "But the stories also say that the Mahika must vow to protect all living creatures. Your heart became evil the moment you convinced yourself that it was okay to take someone's life if it meant saving the moon. It took me a long time to figure it out, but now I see that the Spirits decided to grant the power to someone else." Ligaya smiled. "Me."

I could hardly believe what I was hearing, but it was all starting to make a surreal kind of sense. Ever since she was born, Ligaya had thrived in the outdoors, running through the forest when our mother wasn't looking, and making friends with the oddest creatures. I should have noticed earlier that her affinity for nature bordered on the supernatural.

Mutya's face twisted in grief as she came to the same realization.

"I thought I was doing the right thing," Mutya whispered. "All I ever wanted to do was protect the moon. To protect us."

She sounded so hopeless, I almost felt sorry for her.

"I know." Ligaya's tone softened. "Sometimes, we do evil

things because we think they're the right things to do. But what matters now is how we move forward."

My sister's words took everyone by surprise. We all wanted to give Mutya the punishment she deserved, but Ligaya chose a different path. I felt something kindle in my chest. A fierce, burning pride.

"You were kind to me while we traveled together," Ligaya continued. "You told me all about the different creatures that lived here, from the biggest eagles to the tiniest ants. You told me which plants I could eat when I was hungry, and which ones would make me sick." Ligaya offered Mutya her hand. "I know that you *are* a good person, deep down inside. Come with us, and we can leave this all behind."

A muscle in Mutya's face twitched. No doubt she'd expected to face the datu's merciless justice when she lost the battle, but from her expression, Ligaya's offer of friendship might as well have been a blade tipped with poison. Mutya looked pained, as if that same blade had just pierced deep into her heart.

I knew that feeling, because I had felt it myself when my bakunawa egg lay shattered on the ground.

Perhaps Mutya despised Ligaya because her plan had been thwarted. Or maybe it was because she thought Ligaya had stolen her powers. But most of all, I suspected that in my sister, Mutya saw all the light and goodness that she herself could never be.

With a howl of fury and desolation, Mutya threw herself at my sister, her stone hands outstretched.

As she staggered forward, her face changed. Her skin went from soft and smooth to mottled and wrinkly, her ebony hair turning white as the clouds, as the magic that kept her young all these years finally left her.

Ligaya's eyes widened. At the last moment, a strong gust of wind appeared from nowhere, blowing my sister safely out of the way.

Mutya's howl turned into a scream as her forward momentum carried her right off the cliff. As she fell, the ocean surged. Great Bakunawa opened her jaws and snapped up the old Mahika in one massive gulp.

The scream cut short, and then there was silence.

Chapter 30

Babaylan Kalan-ya let out a strangled cry and ran to the cliff's edge. Swordmaster Pai grabbed the healer's shaking shoulders, holding her back as she stared numbly at the sea.

I turned away from the heart-wrenching sight. Today, a sister had been saved, but so too had one been lost.

Ligaya stared at the place where Mutya had knelt. My sister's face was bloodless. Then she snapped out of her trance, running toward a heap of crumpled feathers on the ground.

The Adarna! Having been so caught up in what just happened, I hadn't even thought to check on the bird that had saved us from the shadow magic.

Ligaya cradled the Adarna in her lap. Its small head hung listlessly in her palm, its feathers faded and dull.

"No," I breathed. "Is it . . . ?"

Ligaya shook her head. "See, its heart is still beating."

The soft feathers above the Adarna's heart fluttered weakly. *Only just.*

Suddenly, I smacked my forehead. "The water from Great Bakunawa's pool!"

I handed Ligaya my container and she trickled a few drops of healing water into the Adarna's beak. My sister's hands trembled. I held my breath as a curious crowd gathered around us.

One of the Adarna's eyes twitched. And then a wing jerked. We watched in rapt wonder as the vibrant color returned to its feathers and the bright, intelligent gleam rekindled in its eyes. With a beat of its wings, the Adarna hopped sprightly onto Ligaya's arm.

Ligaya squealed in delight, engulfing the bird in a one-armed embrace as it nuzzled its head under my sister's chin. I couldn't help but grin.

Before I could check on the injured, I sensed someone approaching from the forest. An old man appeared, his long hair tangled with leaves and his lined face streaked with mud.

I pushed in front of everyone before the Serpent Riders could do anything rash.

"Babaylan Awit!" I called.

The babaylan looked up, growing pale as he saw the armed warriors.

"It's all right. They're my friends." I helped the old man down the ridge until he was seated on a rock. Bato rushed to give him some water, which he gulped down eagerly.

Babaylan Awit frowned as he noticed Bato's scar. "How come you've gotten all scraped up again so soon after I patched you up?"

I was amused to see that the old healer's sharp tongue had returned as soon as he was feeling more refreshed.

"Is this man a friend?" Swordmaster Pai asked.

Kiri nodded excitedly. "Babaylan Awit healed Bato after he almost died fighting a manananggal." With a glare, Bato elbowed Kiri in the ribs.

"Right now, it's *you* we should be worried about," I told the weary babaylan. "What are you doing here, so far from your village?"

I could have bitten my tongue as a shadow passed over Babaylan Awit's face. "With no one but stone statues for company, I couldn't take it anymore. It's been decades since I've made a trip this long, but luckily, my darn-awful sense of direction didn't matter—I simply followed the trail of chaos until I found you."

Seeing the Adarna perched on Ligaya's shoulder, Babaylan Awit said hesitantly, "I was hoping your avian protector could turn my son, and our people, back to how they were."

I bit my lip. I didn't want to get the old man's hopes up, but after his difficult journey, I didn't want to disappoint him either.

To my immense relief, Ligaya was already walking over, evidently having heard our conversation. She tilted her head, listening, as the Adarna chirped in her ear.

"The Adarna sings only what is true," Ligaya said, to

which Babaylan Awit nodded. "Your son was turned to stone to reflect the hardness of his heart, but if he's grown to feel sorry for how he treated you, the Adarna's song should turn him back to flesh and blood."

At my sister's words, the babaylan's eyes shone, this heavy burden lifted from his shoulders.

"Thank you," he said. "Thank you."

"Rest here awhile," Swordmaster Pai offered. "We have food and drink aplenty. Tomorrow, we'll head back to Kalinawan and can pass by your village on the way."

Babaylan Awit took a sweet rice cake from the swordmaster and chewed it with relish.

Leaving him to enjoy his breakfast, I approached Bato and Kiri, standing beneath the broad shade of a coconut tree.

"Did you *see* how Luntian finished off that aswang?" Kiri was saying with enthusiasm. "He made ice out of thin air! Razok flew so high; I didn't know how Luntian could possibly hit him. And then—*bam*! Bull's-eye!"

Bato scoffed. "You thought that was impressive? You should've seen Iska incinerate five aswang with a single breath of fire." Then he grinned. "But . . . that ice spear *was* pretty cool."

After all we had been through, I realized that I now thought of Kiri and Bato as true friends. When we first stepped into the dark forest on the day Ligaya vanished, we were raw novices, even rivals, unsure of our own abilities.

Now we had learned to trust each other.

"Speaking of Iska and Luntian," I asked, "where are they?"

It was odd to see my friends without their loyal bakunawa companions. Instead of replying, Bato pointed to the sea.

Luntian and Iska, along with several other serpents, hovered above the waves. The smaller bakunawa circled Great Bakunawa, keeping their distance, their forked tongues flicking out in suspicion.

I felt a stab of guilt. Because the bakunawa had lived among humans all their lives, they didn't even recognize their own mother.

Brave Iska was the first to muster up her courage. Cautiously, the copper serpent darted closer to Great Bakunawa. I'd always thought Iska was big, but she was easily dwarfed by her mother's looming presence.

Great Bakunawa rippled her tail, and a huge wave rose to send Iska tumbling into the ocean. Iska shot back up, looking affronted—until Luntian spat a stream of water right into Great Bakunawa's face.

A few of the Serpent Riders gasped.

But Great Bakunawa only let out a huff of breath and twitched her fins. With a yelp, Luntian darted away, but wasn't quick enough to avoid getting drenched by another torrent of water. Then Luntian looped back, daring Great Bakunawa to try again.

I blinked in astonishment. *They're playing!*

Sunlight sparkled on scales of myriad colors as all the bakunawa exploded into motion, trying to evade Great

Bakunawa's watery attacks as the mother Serpent swam after her children.

I couldn't believe that this was the same creature who had once struck fear into the hearts of all. What would have been different if the Serpent Riders of centuries past had chosen to understand Great Bakunawa, rather than fight her?

As we watched the serpents chase each other, freer than they'd ever been, I knew in my heart that this was where the wild, elemental bakunawa truly belonged.

It took me a few moments to realize I was smiling.

Chapter 31

I stood on the black shore of Kalinawan, watching the incoming tide swirl around my ankles. Behind me was the sparring ground where I had once competed to become a great warrior.

So much had happened since I last stepped upon these sands. But still, this place felt the same to me.

It felt like home.

Out on the water, a small boat bobbed gently on the waves. The vessel was filled with bolts of fabric, spools of thread, gold jewelry, and jars of dye—basically everything from Ligaya's room. It was a wonder it didn't capsize under all that weight. Everything was securely tied down with vine rope gifted to us by the nuno.

Even now, I couldn't believe that my sister was the Mahika. Because of her newfound magic, Ligaya was obligated to live at Mount Mahiwaga, where she would use her powers to care for the mystical creatures there. Keeping the old stories would have to wait until a new story chanter was born—but I didn't doubt the Spirits would give us one when we needed them.

Ligaya had never been so excited as she was at the thought of living the rest of her life exploring the wild, untamed forest. To her, that was freedom.

Now that the ocean was safe to travel, she planned to leave for the mountain by boat. I was happy for her, yet couldn't help but feel sad that she was leaving so soon.

I turned as someone approached. Babaylan Kalan-ya struggled along the shore, a heavy sack slung across her back. I helped her haul it into the rocking boat. Its contents clinked together, smelling of smoke and herbs.

"Medicines," Babaylan Kalan-ya explained. "No doubt our new Mahika will need them until she learns to make her own."

I nodded. "Thank you. I'm sure Ligaya will appreciate it."

With her errand completed, I expected her to leave, but what she said next surprised me. "You did well, Tanikala. You saved our moon. You brought your sister home."

"I . . . I suppose I did, but it's thanks to everyone that Ligaya is safe."

Suddenly, I remembered her prophecy. "But what did you mean about breaking the chains? I never did that—that was Great Bakunawa."

"Not those metal chains," Babaylan Kalan-ya said. Gently, she placed a finger on my forehead. "The chains in here."

From the village, someone called my name. Ligaya ran

down the sands with the Adarna gliding alongside her. By the time I thought to ask the babaylan what she meant, the old woman had gone.

A lump formed in my throat. This would be the last time I saw my little sister in a long, long while. I swallowed.

"You look wonderful," I said, at a loss for what to say.

Ligaya twirled, showing off her dress that she'd made herself. The multicolored fabric was stitched with gold thread and twinkling golden discs. She looked every inch the princess—or the Mahika—that she was.

Behind my sister, Datu Eeya hurried to catch up. "Are you sure you packed everything?" she called out. "Enough clothes, enough food, enough—"

"Yes, Mother." Ligaya rolled her eyes. "I've triple-checked *everything*."

Our mother gave us one of her rare smiles. "I'm sorry, Ligaya. I still remember holding you in my arms as a tiny baby. I just can't help but worry about you."

"I'll be all—"

Ligaya's words disappeared as our mother suddenly crushed both of us into a tight embrace. With my face pressed against hers, I felt tears tracking down our mother's cheeks.

"My girls," Datu Eeya said, her words muffled in my hair. "My brave warrior girls."

We held each other for a few moments longer.

And then it was time for Ligaya to go.

With Kiri, Bato, and the other Serpent Riders at my side, we gave her our final goodbyes. No sooner had my sister stepped into the boat than the waves moved to do her bidding, bearing her out to sea as fast as a man could row. My sister waved back until we could no longer make out her outline.

As I watched the boat disappear into the horizon, a rainbow streak shot into the clouds and the Adarna let out a joyous cry.

On the horizon, the waves surged. Great Bakunawa rose out of the sea, water cascading down her silver scales. Several smaller bakunawa darted around her—Iska and Luntian among them. Like all the Serpent Riders, Kiri and Bato were devastated when they'd had to part with their loyal bakunawa, but we knew the serpents would be back to visit soon. Everyone was just glad the bakunawa had returned to their true home.

Ligaya's boat was now a mere speck upon the broad mirror of the sea. Despite my sorrow at my sister's departure, I understood that Ligaya had her own path to follow, like we all did. Just as the winds traveled on the courses that the Spirits set, it was only by walking our own paths that we would discover who we truly were.

For so long, I had lived under someone else's shadow, trying to become the person my village wanted me to be—the person I now knew I could never be. But I found my own way to make my mark in the world. I may not have had a bakunawa, but I had my friends, my sword, and my courage. For now, that was enough.

My name was Tanikala. I was the daughter of a datu, sister to the Mahika, and a warrior of Kalinawan.

My story was finally my own.

Acknowledgments

Writing this book was one of the most extraordinary and amazing experiences of my life! Not everyone can say that their Number One Life Dream has come true, and I still can't believe that I'm now one of those people who can. No words will ever be enough to express how incredibly grateful I am to everyone who has helped to shape this story in their own special way.

Firstly and always, *Deo gratias.*

Endless thanks to my agent, Penny Moore, who was one of the first people to read this manuscript and believed in it enough to champion it all this way. Thank you for never giving up on this story.

To my editor, Kei Nakatsuka. From your very first letter, I knew you understood the heart of this story, and you made sure I never lost it through all the rounds of editing. This book (and this author) truly could not have been in better hands and I'm eternally grateful.

Thanks to the team at Bloomsbury Children's who gave this book its perfect publishing home, especially Ariana Abad, Hannah Bowe, Mary Kate Castellani, Erica Chan, Jennifer Choi, Nicholas Church, Beth Eller, Alona Fryman, Emani Glee, Donna Mark, Kathleen Morandini, Andrew Nguyễn, Oona Patrick, Laura Phillips, and Briana Williams. Special thanks also to Vanessa Wojtanowski and Katharine Wiencke. Thank you all for the amazing work you do in getting more books into the hands of young readers!

To Alexis Young, who illustrated the cover, and Yelena Safronova for the book design. I still can't get over the fact that you took on my little story and created such a beautiful and magical work of art. I'm so, so grateful for the time and talent you gave to this project.

Nanay and Tats, thank you for taking little me on all the trips to the library. Thank you for always believing I could write a book even when I didn't, and for possibly being more excited about this story getting published than I was. This all would not exist without the sacrifices you made for me. I hope I've made you proud.

Elyxa and Yxaak, you always laugh at me but are always there for me when I need it most. Thank you for reading my early manuscripts with the care and brutal honesty that only little siblings have. You guys are the best.

To the Tan-Magno family, especially Lola Linda, Ninang Marlene, Ninang Gigi, Ninang Marie, and all my titos and cousins, for surrounding me with love and many, many books. And to the Vega-Diño family, especially Lola Norma,

Lolo Forts, Ninang Beng, Ninang Jing, Ninang Leng, and all my titos and cousins, for all the adventures through the mountains, forests, beaches, and rivers of our home.

To my supportive and encouraging friends, especially Jo Cadiz, for always sticking with me despite all the years that have passed and the four thousand miles of ocean between us. To my elementary school teacher, Ms. Mitch, who was the first person who told me I could be a writer, and ensured I never forgot where I came from. To the GHS Class of 2019, for all the support you gave to this bookish girl and for letting me be myself.

Finally, to you, dear reader. It's so surreal to know that a story that previously existed only in my head is now in your hands. Thank you for embarking on this adventure, and I hope you enjoyed the journey. *Hanggang sa muli!*

Yxavel Magno Diño was born in the Philippines before moving to Australia at a young age, where she soon discovered that almost nobody there knew how to say her name. To make up for it, she spent her time daydreaming about fantasy worlds filled with characters who had more unusual names than she did. Now, she writes stories about her Filipino heritage and its fantastical folklore. When she's not writing, you can find her drinking copious amounts of black tea or getting lost in the pages of a book.

ymdino.com
@yxavel_writes